NO PL

A bullet buzzed past his hair, struck one of the teens, and sent it spinning off the wall.

Longarm let his instincts do the reacting for him. He flung himself to the left in a rolling dive. Even as he was rolling over on the sand, his hand found the butt of his Colt and palmed the revolver out of the cross-draw rig on his left hip.

But there was nothing to shoot at. He saw nothing but sand, no   zard could be up there on   any of those dunes.

With a vicious whine, another bullet whipped past his ear. Longarm couldn't be sure, but he thought this shot came from a different direction. He saw a puff of white smoke from the crest of a dune to his left and snapped a shot toward it. Then a fourth slug smacked into the wall just to his right.

They had him in a crossfire.

DON'T MISS THESE
ALL-ACTION WESTERN SERIES
FROM THE BERKLEY PUBLISHING GROUP

THE GUNSMITH by J. R. Roberts
Clint Adams was a legend among lawmen, outlaws and ladies.
They called him . . . the Gunsmith.

LONGARM by Tabor Evans
The popular long-running series about Deputy U.S. Marshal
Long—his life, his loves, his fight for justice.

SLOCUM by Jake Logan
Today's longest-running action Western. John Slocum rides
a deadly trail of hot blood and cold steel.

BUSHWHACKERS by B. J. Lanagan
An action-packed series by the creators of Longarm! The
rousing adventures of the most brutal gang of cutthroats ever
assembled—Quantrill's Raiders.

DIAMONDBACK by Guy Brewer
Dex Yancey is Diamondback, a Southern gentleman turned
con man when his brother cheats him out of the family for-
tune. Ladies love him. Gamblers hate him. But nobody pulls
one over on Dex . . .

WILDGUN by Jack Hanson
The blazing adventures of mountain man Will Barlow—from
the creators of Longarm!

TEXAS TRACKER by Tom Calhoun
Meet J. T. Law: the most relentless—and dangerous—
manhunter in all Texas. Where sheriffs and posses fail, he's
the best man to bring in the most vicious outlaws—for a
price.

TABOR EVANS

LONGARM

AND THE DESERT ROSE

JOVE BOOKS, NEW YORK

This is a work of fiction. Names, characters, places, and incidents either are the product of the author's imagination or are used fictitiously, and any resemblance to actual persons, living or dead, business establishments, events, or locales is entirely coincidental.

LONGARM AND THE DESERT ROSE

A Jove Book / published by arrangement with
the author

PRINTING HISTORY
Jove edition / January 2003

Copyright © 2003 by Penguin Putnam Inc.

Visit our website at
www.penguinputnam.com

ISBN: 0-515-13442-2

A JOVE BOOK®
Jove Books are published by The Berkley Publishing Group,
a division of Penguin Putnam Inc.,
375 Hudson Street, New York, New York 10014.
JOVE and the "J" design
are trademarks belonging to Penguin Putnam Inc.

PRINTED IN THE UNITED STATES OF AMERICA

10 9 8 7 6 5 4 3 2 1

Chapter 1

He dreamed, and in his dream he was making love with the woman again. Her name was Elizabeth, and she had thick, dark brown hair that fell in wings around her lovely face. As she lowered her head over his groin, he ran his fingers through her hair. When she opened her mouth and took his erect shaft into it, his hands tightened a little on her head in reaction before he remembered that most women didn't like that and forced his fingers to relax. She closed her lips around his throbbing member and ran her tongue around the crown, then used the tip to toy with the opening and lap up the juices that already were welling from him. He closed his eyes and lay back to enjoy the delicious sensations she was creating within him.

For several minutes, he didn't move, just sprawled there on the bed and let Elizabeth work her magic with her lips and tongue and the fingers that stole to the inside of his thighs to massage and caress the muscles there. Lazily, he reached out and placed a hand on her back, moving it up and down and enjoying the smooth sleekness of her skin under his palm. She was as skilled at what she was doing as any woman he had ever met, and he had bedded a good many over the years, both before and since leaving West-

1

by-God Virginia to come to the frontier following the Late Unpleasantness.

It would have been easy just to wait for his climax to overwhelm him and spill his seed in that hot mouth of hers, but that wasn't what he wanted. She deserved more than that. So, after a while, an interval of some of the most tantalizing pleasure he had ever known, he grasped her shoulders and urged her up over him. She didn't argue. She was smiling as she let the thick pole of male flesh slide out of her mouth. Moving with catlike grace, she straddled his hips and poised there for a moment, letting him look up at her and drink in her beauty. His hands went to her apple-sized breasts and he cupped the mounds of warm, creamy femininity. His thumbs stroked the hard, cherry red nipples. Elizabeth's eyes were dark and hooded with desire. She reached underneath her, closed her fingers around his erection, and guided it into her as she sank down on him. The pace of their joining was deliberate, as if they both wanted to make this coupling last and draw as much joy from it as they could.

"My God," she breathed. "There's so much of you to take in. But I want it all, every last bit."

Finally, his shaft was embedded all the way inside her. She gave a long sigh of satisfaction, obviously pleased with herself that she had been able to take him. For almost a minute, she sat there, motionless, her eyes half-closed, while he continued toying with her breasts and let her grow accustomed to the feeling of fullness he created in her. Then her hips began to move, slowly at first but then with a growing urgency and speed. She leaned forward, resting her lithe, petite body on his broad, muscular chest and found his mouth with hers. Her lips were open, ready for his tongue to slide between them and penetrate her for the second time. Her hips bounced up and down, and he met her thrusts with his own, his hips rising from the mattress and then falling as he drove his shaft in and out of her.

Their level of passion was so high, so intense, that there was no way either of them could stand it for very long. Within minutes they were breathing hard and thrusting and driving and clutching at each other. He reached down and caught hold of her hips to steady her as he pounded into her, his massive organ penetrating deeper and deeper as excitement made her womanhood open even more to him. His groin was drenched with the dew that emanated from her. They were as slick and hot and wet as a man and a woman could be.

She shuddered and cried out as her culmination washed over her. He froze where he was, letting the buttery muscles of her femininity quake around him, and that sensation sent him plummeting over the edge as well. His seed raced from the heavy sacs between his legs up his shaft and then erupted into her in white-hot spurts. He emptied himself inside her, leaving him drained and gasping for breath. She went limp atop him, every bit as satiated as he was.

It just didn't get any better than that. No how, no way.

But then, through the golden afterglow of the dream, pain hit him, stabs of agony that shot through his body and made it jerk and spasm. The heat of lovemaking went away, to be replaced by a grim coldness that sent shivers up and down his spine. With the pain and the cold came awareness. The dream had been nice, but it was only a dream. He would never make love to Elizabeth again.

She was dead. And that bastard Culhane had killed her.

He sank back against the pillow and felt a blanket underneath him. Trying to force the pain to the back of his mind, Longarm opened his eyes and wondered where the hell he was—and who that woman was who had both hands wrapped around his talleywhacker.

• • •

3

The sky outside had been gray with the approach of dawn that morning when Sarah Hodge heard her dog barking behind the house. Dobie was the sort that barked at everything and nothing, but Sarah thought there was some extra urgency in the sound this time. Snakes crawled up from time to time in this settlement where the high desert turned into the mountains, short fat diamondback rattlers that packed plenty of venom in their bite. Sarah knew that dogs, unlike humans, seldom died from snakebites, but she didn't want to take a chance that Dobie had some rattler coiled up in a corner, ready to strike. He was a small dog. She got out of bed in her cotton nightgown, shrugged into a robe and went out of the bedroom and through the kitchen to the back door. Before opening the door, she picked up the Winchester that leaned in a nearby corner and levered a cartridge into the rifle's chamber. She'd been able to shoot the head off a snake since she was twelve years old, and that was a decade in the past.

Sarah pulled open the door and called, "Dobie? Dobie, where are you?"

The barking sounded like it was coming from the shed where Sarah kept the mare that pulled her buggy. Dobie was really upset about something. Sarah moved down onto the split logs that formed the rear steps, then hesitated as she realized she was barefooted. If there was a snake crawling around, she didn't want to go out there with no shoes on. She went back into the kitchen and placed the rifle on the butcher block. A pair of boots sat beside the door. She picked them up one by one and shook them out, checking for scorpions. None of the vicious little creatures fell out. Sarah jammed her feet into the boots, brushed her blond hair back away from her face with her fingers, and picked up the Winchester again. She probably looked a sight, she thought, her hair tangled from sleep, wearing nightclothes and boots and carrying a rifle. But nobody was liable to be up and about this

4

early in the morning, so she really didn't care. She went outside and walked across the yard toward the shed. A few beads of moisture clung to the sparse blades of grass. It got cold here at night, even in the summer like this, but the air was so dry hardly any dew formed.

"All right, Dobie, settle down," Sarah said as she approached the shed. "Even if there's a rattlesnake back there, there's no need to pitch such a conniption fit."

The dog kept on barking. Sarah shook her head and stepped around the corner of the shed.

She gasped and jerked back as she saw the dark figure leaning against the rear wall of the shed. The light wasn't strong enough yet for her to be able to make out any details, but the shape was tall and broad and menacing. Sarah's first thought was of the Cheyenne renegades who sometimes rode through the small strip of fertile ground that separated the desert from the mountains, but she could tell somehow that this man was not an Indian. He slumped against the wall as if he were exhausted or hurt or both. His head drooped forward, even though he was on his feet. Was he unconscious? He wasn't moving. Sarah lifted the rifle anyway, just in case he did move, and said, "Who are you? What do you want here?"

The man lifted his head a little. He had heard her. He wasn't unconscious after all. But he wasn't coherent, either. The best he could do was let out a groan.

Sarah wished she had a lamp. A cottonwood tree grew beside the shed, making the predawn shadows back here even thicker. She sidled away, keeping the rifle trained on the stranger. "If you're hurt, I'll try to help you," she said. "I can go get Doc Barkley. But you've got to come out here where I can get a look at you."

With both hands braced against the wall to steady him, the man took a couple of steps forward. Then his balance deserted him and he swayed forward. Too weak to catch himself, he toppled to the ground, groaning again when he landed hard on his side. Sarah gave a small, involuntary cry as she flinched away from him. In only seconds, though, her natural boldness—that bane of her parents' existence when she was younger—asserted itself, and she moved toward the man as he lay on the ground near the shed.

"Don't you move," she told him. "I've got a Winchester here, and I know how to use it. I don't mind using it, either."

If he heard her, he gave no sign of it. Maybe now he really had passed out, she told herself as she approached.

The sun was peeking over the horizon now, and her eyes had adjusted to the weak light. She saw that the man was dressed like a cowhand, in denim trousers and jacket and a butternut shirt. The fabric of that shirt showed a dark, ragged stain where the stranger's jacket hung open. He had no hat, and his boots were too low-heeled to be a cowboy's. A leather gunbelt was strapped around his waist. He was lying on his right side, so she could see that the holster attached to the belt rode on the left, and a pistol with plain walnut grips was snugged into the holster with the butt facing forward for a cross-draw.

So the stranger was some sort of gunman, not a cowboy, Sarah told herself. No doubt he had been wounded in a fight with some other pistolero. Not that too many of that sort of men came through here. Bell City was small and peaceful, a haven from the violence that seemed to infest so much of the rest of the frontier. Sheriff Clyde Hampton didn't stand for interlopers making trouble in his town.

The proximity of the Circle C ranch helped, too. The crew of the Circle C was a salty bunch, and they would have come down like a ton of bricks on any troublemaker they encountered.

What she ought to do, Sarah told herself, was to back away from this wounded man and run down to Sheriff

Hampton's office. The sheriff could get Doc Barkley and come along to deal with this. That was their job, after all, dealing with violent men and the damage they did to each other.

The little dog was still barking, and the shrill sounds finally got on Sarah's nerves. "Dobie, hush up!" she snapped. He gave her an offended look and backed away, then turned back toward the stranger and growled.

Sarah shivered. It would be plenty hot later, but right now there was a definite chill in the air. The wounded man had lost enough blood so that he probably felt even colder.

She made up her mind. She would get the man into the house and then fetch the sheriff. Anyway, she couldn't very well go running down the main street of Bell City in her nightclothes. She would get dressed first, too.

She reached down with the barrel of the Winchester and prodded the shoulder of the wounded man. He didn't stir, didn't even make a sound this time. Sarah leaned the rifle against the wall of the shed and bent over to slide her hands under his arms. She grunted with effort as she tried to lift some of his weight off the ground. He was a big man. Not fat by any means, actually sort of rangy except for those broad shoulders, but he packed plenty of meat on his long, tall frame. She eased his shoulders down and went around to take his feet instead. That worked better, although she worried about what dragging his torso over the ground might do to the wound in his side.

The sun was up, a blinding red-orange orb over the desert to the east, by the time Sarah got the stranger to the back door. None of her neighbors were out and about yet, though, or she would have called to them for help. She couldn't drag the man up the steps. She had to push and pull him into a sitting position beside them and sort of *roll* him up and through the door. Then, she was able to take his feet and drag him into her bedroom. She frowned at the smears of blood he left behind on the plank flooring. She would have a devil of a time getting those stains up.

She spread an old but clean blanket on the bed before she lifted him onto it, so that he wouldn't get blood on the sheets. Raising him onto the bed was the hardest chore yet, and when she was finished with it she was breathing hard and had beads of sweat on her face despite the cool, early morning air in the room. The clicking of toenails on the floor behind her told her that Dobie had followed her into the room. The little dog whined.

"I know, I know," Sarah said. "You don't have to tell me it was foolish of me to bring him in here. You know what Brent always says, that I'm too softhearted for my own good. But I couldn't just leave him lying out there on the ground. I'll get dressed now and go find Sheriff Hampton."

She started to turn away from the bed, but then she turned back and reached down to unbuckle the gunbelt. She felt uncomfortable with the man wearing it in her bed. She was able to work it out from under him. Coiling the belt, she placed it and the holster and the gun on a dressing table across the room.

She went to her wardrobe and opened it, then hesitated again. She felt a little odd about getting undressed with this strange man right here in the room with her, even though he seemed to be out cold. Stepping over to the bed, she looked down at him, studying his face intently to make sure he wasn't shamming. It was a strong face, handsome in a rough-hewn way, mostly planes and angles and high cheekbones that gave him a vaguely Indian look. His skin had been weathered and darkened by years of exposure to the elements until it was the same brown color as old saddle leather. He wore a mustache, a thick, luxurious growth that swept out to both sides of his mouth and curled upward, reminding Sarah of the horns of a

8

longhorn steer. His hair was dark brown, like the mahogany of a piano. After a few moments, Sarah decided that he really was unconscious. She went back to the wardrobe, took off the wrapper, then pulled the nightgown over her head. A smile tugged at the corners of her mouth. She must have looked pretty humorous, standing there naked except for a pair of man's boots.

The stranger picked that moment to moan again.

Sarah's head snapped around. Plenty of light came into the room through the gauzy curtains over the windows by now, and she saw that the man's eyes were still closed. He hadn't waked up and seen her. Quickly, she reached into the wardrobe and picked out some clothes, pulling them on in a hurry. When she was dressed, she ran her fingers through her hair again and turned toward the bedroom door, intending to go out and bring in the rifle, then head for town and the sheriff and doctor.

The stranger started to shift around on the bed, his movements slow, jerky, and evidently causing him pain. Sarah went to him. Maybe she could ease him a bit, make him more comfortable before she left. She pulled off his boots and dropped them on the floor next to the bed. Her eyes went to the buckle of his belt and the buttons that fastened his trousers. The wound was on his right side, about halfway up his torso, and though the blood had soaked his shirt, it hadn't spread to his trousers. She could get them off of him as well and then cover him with another blanket. She didn't want to try to remove his jacket and shirt because she was afraid she would hurt him worse. Doc Barkley would have to attend to that.

Taking a man's pants off wasn't something she had that much practice at, she thought as she fumbled with the buckle and the buttons. It wasn't like she was some blushing, completely innocent schoolgirl. Almost, but not quite. She got the belt unbuckled and the trousers unbuttoned, and she went to the foot of the bed to tug them down his legs, leaving him clad from the waist down in socks and the bottom half of a pair of long underwear.

It was summerweight underwear, not too thick, and she had no trouble seeing the male appendages clustered at the bottom of his groin. In fact, the front of the underwear reminded her of a tent, the way it was standing up. Sarah felt her face growing warm. She knew what it meant when a man looked like that. He was excited. Even wounded, perhaps in danger of his life, his organ had become erect.

That couldn't be good for him, especially considering that he had already lost so much blood. He moaned again, and she asked herself if it was from pain this time—or from lust?

Just as when he had been lying unconscious by the shed, she couldn't leave him like this. She leaned over the bed, and with trembling fingers she began unfastening the buttons on the underwear. As soon as there was a large enough opening, his manhood practically sprang through it in such a forceful exit that she jumped back, catching her breath.

This was the first . . . *thing* . . . she had seen in such a state of arousal, unless you counted animals. It was certainly large, and it seemed to grow even larger before her eyes, until it was so long and thick she couldn't imagine it being able to enter a woman's body without ripping her apart. She became aware that she was lifting her hand. She stopped herself before she could reach out and touch it, shocked that she would even consider doing such a thing, especially under the circumstances. The man was injured, after all, and as for her . . . well, this was hardly the time for her to be fondling a strange man's sexual equipment. Not that there would ever be a proper time for such scandalous behavior.

The man growled deep in his throat and moved his hips so that his shaft thrust up even higher in the air. She couldn't have him writhing around like that, Sarah decided. Such frenzied motions were liable to make his injury worse. And she could think of only one way to ease the state in which he found himself. What she was about to do was strictly for medical, humanitarian purposes.

She took a deep breath and reached out with both hands, wrapping her fingers around the thick pole of engorged flesh.

She was stunned at how hot it was and how hard it had become, yet soft at the same time, like a bar of iron sheathed in velvet. Acting purely on instinct, she began to move her hands up and down. The man groaned again, and he said something, his voice thick and difficult to understand. Sarah thought the word sounded like "Elizabeth." That had to be the name of the woman he was with inside his mind, where a scene from his memory—or from some flight of fancy—was playing itself out. Sarah kept sliding her hands along his shaft. A bead of moisture appeared at the tip, and as she brought her hands back up, more of the clear juice pearled out. She used a fingertip to spread it around, marveling at how slick it was. Then she went back to pumping his manhood, bringing him closer and closer to climax.

When the moment arrived, she was shocked again at the intensity of it. His pole swelled even more and throbbed heavily in her hands as it unleashed its power. She didn't rub anymore, just held tight, feeling as if she were holding the horn of a saddle strapped to the back of a bucking bronco. Holding on for dear life. As his spasms dwindled to a final few twitches, she became aware of the wetness between her legs. Again her face burned with shame—but it was not nearly as hot as the fire that blazed deep inside her.

It was at that moment she became aware that he was awake and staring at her in confusion. She looked at him, looked down at what she was holding in her hands . . .

And screamed.

Chapter 2

It had all started simply, as it so often did. Longarm had strolled into the federal building on Colfax Avenue in Denver on a beautiful summer morning—a little late, as usual, but not too much—and Henry, the pasty-faced young gent who played the typewriter in the outer office of Chief Marshal Billy Vail, told Longarm that Vail wanted to see him. "Pronto," Henry added.

Longarm stopped, a cheroot tilted at a jaunty angle between his teeth. "Pronto?" he repeated. "Damn, Henry, I reckon you've finally been out here long enough you're starting to sound like a real human being instead of an Easterner."

"Just go on in," Henry snapped. "He'll give you an assignment and then you can leave, but I have to stay here and listen to him complain about how late and how insubordinate you are and—"

"I reckon I get the drift," Longarm broke in with a grin. He opened the door and went into Vail's inner office.

The chief marshal didn't look all that upset, Longarm thought as he sat down in the red leather chair in front of the desk, cocked his right ankle on his left knee, and dropped his flat-crowned, snuff brown Stetson on the floor beside the chair. He had seen Vail looking a lot more apoplectic than he did now. Longarm took the cheroot out of his mouth and said, "Mornin', Billy."

"Is it?" Vail asked, his voice mild. "I would have sworn it was past noon by now."

Longarm glanced at the banjo clock on the wall. "Nope. Just nine-thirty."

Vail nodded. Pudgy, balding, and pink-cheeked, he had been one hell-roarer of a lawman in his day, serving as a Texas Ranger and a deputy United States marshal before he'd started riding a desk as the chief marshal in the Denver office. He could still fork a bronc and pack iron if he had to, but such occasions were few and far between. Mostly he sent out his deputies on their assignments and went home to his wife at the end of the day, which probably accounted for the wistful look Longarm saw in his eyes every now and then.

"Got a job for you, Custis," Vail went on, picking up some papers from the welter of documents scattered on his desk. "Ever hear of Rampart Valley?"

Longarm blew a smoke ring and then asked, "Over west of here a ways, ain't it?"

"That's right. Good ranching country. The railroad went through there a while back, made it boom even more."

Longarm nodded in understanding. The arrival of the steel rails and the iron horse had made a lot of good country even better for ranchers.

"Somebody's been holding up the trains over there," Vail continued. "They stop the train, bust open the cattle cars, and run off the stock."

"Rustling cattle off a train?" Longarm said with a frown. "I never heard of such a thing. Don't see as how it falls under federal jurisdiction, though."

"It wouldn't except that the gang hits the express cars

13

at the same time. They've carried off several bags of mail. That makes it Uncle Sam's business."

Longarm nodded again. "And the local star packers, who ain't been able to find hide nor hair of the rustlers, were only too glad to pass the chore along to us," he guessed.

"That's about the size of it," Vail confirmed. "Here's the report I got from a lawman over there name of Willard." He handed Longarm the papers he had picked up a few minutes earlier. "You can read it on the train while you're on your way to Castleton. That's the main settlement in Rampart Valley."

"Nobody has any idea who these wideloopers are?"

"Nary a one. It'll be up to you to find out."

Longarm dropped the butt of his cheroot on the floor in front of the chair and ground it out under his boot heel. "Sure, Billy. I've done this sort of job before." He picked up his hat and got to his feet.

"There's just one more little thing, Custis," Vail said.

Longarm paused as he started to turn toward the door. "What's that, Billy?"

A brick red hue was stealing over Vail's face, and Longarm realized his boss had been holding in his anger until after business was taken care of. Vail put his hands flat on the desk, pushed himself to his feet, and bellowed, "If you ever come waltzing in here thirty minutes late again without a damned good reason, I'll nail your hide to the wall so fast you'll still be wearing it!"

Longarm had witnessed dozens of these tirades from Vail, so he didn't take it personally. He said, "I had a good reason, Billy."

"Oh?" Vail said, so angry now he was trembling. "And what was that?"

"A run of some of the best poker hands you ever saw, down at the Golden Slipper last night."

"Let me get this straight," Vail said. "Playing cards half

14

the night in some saloon is a good excuse for coming to work late the next day?"

Longarm pursed his lips. "Well . . . not as good as a pretty woman, I reckon, but almost."

Vail was still cussing at the top of his lungs when Longarm slipped out of the office a few moments later. He grinned at Henry, who sat at his typewriter with a wide-eyed, horrified look on his bespectacled face.

"There you go," said Longarm. "I got him all warmed up for you."

He caught a train that afternoon for Cheyenne, and after a layover of a couple of hours during which he got himself some supper and a drink of Maryland rye in a saloon near the depot, the westbound came in and Longarm boarded it. He would have to sleep sitting up, since the train wouldn't get to Castleton until the middle of the next day and the marshal's office wouldn't pay for him to travel in a sleeping compartment. Longarm would have had to make up the difference in the cost himself, and it was close enough to the end of the month that he didn't have that sort of money right now.

He put the time to good use, reading once again through the papers Billy Vail had given him. The sheriff in Castleton was named Stan Willard, and according to his report, three trains loaded with cattle eastbound from Castleton had been stopped in the past six months. The cattle had been unloaded from the trains by a gang of masked rustlers and owlhoots and driven off, never to be seen again. While they had the trains stopped, the outlaws had cleaned out the express car each time, too, but that seemed to the witnesses like something of an afterthought. When Willard had been notified of the unorthodox rustling, he had gathered a posse and tried to trail the stolen herds. It had been easy enough to pick up the trail—it was damned near impossible to move hundreds of cattle without leaving some sign—but it had circled to the southwest and come to an abrupt end at the edge of the *Llano Caliente,* a strip of hellish, waterless desert some forty miles wide. The tracks vanished there, swallowed up by the ever-shifting sands. It seemed impossible to believe that a herd of cattle could be driven across the *Llano Caliente,* but all the evidence indicated that was what had happened.

Longarm sighed when he read Sheriff Willard's comments about the desert. He had been to plenty of deserts in the past—Death Valley, the Mojave, the Painted Desert, the Sonoran Desert down in Mexico, the nameless sandhills of West Texas—and he hadn't liked any of them. He had come too damned close to dying in all of those places for that.

The first step in catching the rustlers would be figuring out where they had taken those stolen cows. Longarm figured he would have to rent or buy a horse when he got to Castleton so he could do some poking around the *Llano Caliente.* That meant "hot plains" in Spanish, and he suspected it lived up to its name.

When Longarm had gleaned everything he could from the reports, he folded them up and slipped them into an inner pocket in his brown tweed coat. Then he took out a cheroot, fished a lucifer from another pocket, and snapped the match into life with an iron-hard thumbnail. While he was smoking the cheroot, a porter came through the car and turned down the lamps so that the passengers would have an easier time sleeping. Of course, nobody was going to get much restful slumber on a hard wooden bench. Longarm finished his smoke, leaned back, tilted his hat down over his eyes, and sighed.

The gentle rocking motion of a train that was so conducive to sleep when a gent was stretched out in a compartment just served to annoy one who was sitting up. Still, Longarm dozed off after a while, and he found himself in a particularly vivid dream. He was out in the desert, and the burning sands were so hot he could only skip along, yelping each time one of his feet came down. When he looked ahead of him, he saw a herd of cattle receding into the distance. Longarm yelled, "Hey!" and ran after them, but he couldn't seem to catch up. After a while, the cattle looked back at him, and damned if the brutes weren't laughing. They thought it was so blasted funny that he was chasing them. Angered, Longarm yanked his Colt from its holster and blazed away at them, but every time he pulled the trigger, no bullets came out, only spurts of sand. Longarm cussed, shook the gun, and fired again, and this time instead of a bullet, a big drop of blood welled from the muzzle of the Colt and plopped onto the sand at his feet. He stared in amazement at the gun as more blood oozed from the barrel and the cylinder and dripped down over his hand. Amazement changed to horror.

He came awake with a jerk and found himself sitting on the same bench where he had gone to sleep earlier. The train was still rolling along, headed west. Longarm sat up, stretched his neck to ease a crick, and looked around. Everybody else in the car seemed to be asleep. Not wanting to fall right back into that nightmare if he dozed off again, he decided to stay awake for a while. To keep his mind occupied, he thought back over his life, trying to remember all the gals he had bedded, starting when he was just a kid back in West-by-God Virginia. To his chagrin, he couldn't even remember the name of the first one.

Somewhere during the night, he fell asleep again, and this time there were no nightmares.

Several cups of coffee in the train's dining car helped wake him up the next morning, but he was still tired and his eyes were gritty as he stepped off onto the platform of the Castleton depot around midday. He looked around and saw that he was one of only three passengers disembarking from the train, and no one seemed to be getting on. He walked down to the baggage car and reclaimed his warbag, saddle, and Winchester, then went over to the ticket window. "Where can I find the sheriff's office?" he asked the slick-haired gent behind the wicket.

"There's not any trouble, I hope?" the ticket agent asked. "Was something wrong on the train?"

"Rest easy, old son," Longarm assured him. "Everything was fine. My business with the sheriff ain't got anything to do with your railroad."

The agent nodded in relief. "In that case, go out the front door of the station, go straight for a block, and then turn left. Sheriff Willard's office and the jail will be three blocks down on your left."

"Much obliged," Longarm said. He left the depot and followed the agent's directions, finding himself on Castleton's broad, dusty main street.

The settlement was a typical Western cowtown, the same sort as hundreds of others that Longarm had visited. Maybe a little more civilized than some, because in addition to a heap of saloons and dance halls and gambling dens, Castleton also had several churches and a school. Those developments had probably come with the railroad. Business was always the first element to arrive in a new town, followed closely—sometimes hand in hand—by sin. Religion and education came last. That pattern had been repeated countless times as the country spread across the continent and doubtless would continue to do so.

Longarm found the sheriff's office without any trouble. It was located in the front, frame section of a good-sized building, the rear two-thirds of which were made of stone. That would be the jail part, Longarm reasoned. The door of the sheriff's office was unlocked. He went in and found a ruggedly built, white-haired man of late middle age standing beside a black cast-iron stove, pouring himself a cup of coffee. The lawman turned a weathered face toward Longarm. "Mornin'," he said. "Help you with something?"

"Sheriff Willard?" Longarm asked.

"That's right."

"I'm Deputy U.S. Marshal Custis Long, out of the Denver office." Longarm reached inside his coat. "I got my badge and bona fides right here."

He handed over the leather folder he took from his pocket. Willard opened it and looked at the identification long enough to be satisfied, but not so long that he seemed overly suspicious. As he handed the folder back to Longarm, he said, "Pleased to meet you, Marshal. I reckon you're here because of the reports I sent to Marshal Vail about those train robberies."

"Yep," Longarm said.

Willard lifted his coffee cup and raised his eyebrows in a question.

"I'd be much obliged for a cup," Longarm said. "But only if it's good and strong. Didn't sleep much on the train last night."

"I never sleep worth a damn on a train," Willard said as he set his own cup aside, picked up another from a shelf next to the stove, and used a piece of thick leather as a potholder while he poured coffee for Longarm. "This stuff's so stout you can use it to patch a hole in a roof if you let it set for a while."

Longarm grinned. "Sounds like just what I need."

The two lawmen took their coffee and adjourned to the desk, Willard sitting behind it in a battered old swivel chair, Longarm taking a ladder-back chair in front of it. The coffee was as potent as Willard boasted, and a few sips of the black, bitter brew did more to revive him than what he'd had on the train.

"I realize I got you over here on false pretenses, Mar-

19

shal," Willard said with a rueful grin. "I just haven't had any luck finding those rustlers."

"Not at all. Those boys interfered with the United States mail. That makes 'em federal criminals, too."

Willard grunted. "They should've stuck to widelooping cows."

"I reckon you'd've picked up their trail sooner or later," Longarm said. He felt an instinctive liking for Willard, sensing that the man was a good small-town star packer.

"Maybe, maybe not. That *Llano Caliente* is a big chunk of nothing. It swallowed up those stolen cows like they were never there."

Longarm took another sip of his coffee, then leaned forward to ask, "What's on the other side of that desert? Those rustlers have to be going *somewhere*. It ain't the desert that's their final destination."

"That's true enough," Willard agreed. "The *Llano Caliente* is about forty miles across and runs for a good ninety miles north and south. On the other side, it backs up to some mountains, a little range called the Solomons. There's a strip of decent land between the desert and the mountains, just big enough to support a few ranches."

"Any settlements?"

"A place called Bell City," Willard replied.

"Maybe that's where the rustlers are taking those beeves," Longarm suggested.

The sheriff shook his head. "There's no market there for them. The railroad doesn't go to Bell City, though there's been talk of building a spur line up there from the south. Right now, though, from Bell City they'd have to be either driven over the mountains to the west or back across the desert to the east."

Longarm frowned. "You said there were already ranches over there. What do they do with their stock?"

"They drive south to the nearest rail line. There's a

20

junction called Rossville, 'bout seventy-five miles south of Bell City."

"Then why couldn't the rustlers take the cattle there and sell them?"

"They could," Willard allowed, "but I've been in touch with the law over there and the fella who runs the stockyard, know both of them well. They say there hasn't been any strange stock brought there in the past six months, and they'd know about it if it had been."

"If there are ranchers in that strip, the rustled beeves could be going through them. Change a few brands and nobody would be suspicious if those cattlemen are already bringing their stock to Rossville."

Again, Willard shook his head. "I thought of that, too. But according to the gents I know over there, none of the local ranchers have shipped out any more stock than what they already had on hand. Nobody's had a sudden increase in his herd."

Longarm drained the rest of the coffee and took out a cheroot. From the sound of what Willard was telling him, the sheriff had already considered and eliminated most of the possibilities concerning the disposal of the stolen cattle. But those cows had to be going somewhere, and when Longarm found them, he would also find the men wanted for stealing the U.S. mail.

Willard clasped knobby-knuckled hands together in front of him. "Anyway, this whole palaver is putting the cart before the horse, Marshal. There's no way anybody could drive those cattle across the desert. Not forty miles without water."

"There are no water holes at all out there?"

"None that I know of," Willard said. "Of course, I can't say that I've ridden every square inch of the *Llano Caliente*. Nobody around here has, as far as I know. But I've been in this part of the country for over twenty years, and I never heard-tell of any water holes. There used to be quite a few Indians around these parts—still get a few Cheyenne riding through every now and then—and if anybody would know about water in the desert, it's them. But they don't start across the *Llano Caliente* without packing plenty of water with them, either."

"And nobody could carry enough water with them to satisfy a herd of thirsty cows," Longarm mused. "But that's where the tracks led."

Willard sighed and nodded. "It's a vexation, all right, Marshal. It's like they vanished into thin air. I wish you better luck than I had in finding them."

Longarm thought for a moment, then asked, "Is there any law in Bell City?"

"Yeah. The sheriff's name is Clyde Hampton."

"Good man?"

"Seems to be," Willard said. "I don't really know him that well. Only met him a few times, in fact. But I haven't heard any complaints about him."

Longarm had been toying with his empty coffee cup as he chewed the end of the unlit cheroot. Now he set the cup on the desk and stood up. "Reckon I'll be doing some riding, getting to know the lay of the land around here. Is there a good livery in town?"

"Sure is. Townsend's, two blocks west on the other side of the street."

"Much obliged, Sheriff."

"Tell Elizabeth I sent you."

Longarm paused in the act of turning toward the door. He looked at Willard and raised his eyebrows. "Elizabeth? The stable's run by a woman?"

"She took it over after her pa got down and couldn't work anymore. Always was quite a tomboy, so she took right to it. To tell you the truth, I figure she's got a better eye for horseflesh than her old man ever did."

Longarm nodded. "That's good. I'll need a dependable

horse if I'm going out into that desert to find those rustlers."

"You'll need more than that," Willard said, his face solemn. "You'll need plenty of water—and even more luck."

Chapter 3

Longarm walked through the open double doors of the livery stable and looked around. The wide aisle down the middle of the barn was empty, as were the office to the left and the tack room to the right. The doors of both were open so that he could see inside. He heard horses moving around in some of the stalls. He was about to call out and ask if anyone was there when movement caught his eye. He lifted his gaze to the hayloft that lay above the stalls in the rear half of the barn. At first he wasn't sure what he was looking at, but then he recognized it as a trim, nicely rounded rear end clad in tight denim trousers. Somebody was bending over up there, probably forking up some hay. Longarm hoped like hell it was Elizabeth Townsend and not some fella who worked for her. Otherwise he was going to feel mighty foolish about staring at that rump.

The next moment, both of his hunches were confirmed, because the person with the pitchfork straightened and pitched a big chunk of hay toward the ground below. Longarm caught a glimpse of thick dark hair around a pretty face, as well as nice breasts under a flannel shirt, before he had to jump back to keep the hay from landing on his head.

"Oh, my God! Are you all right?" The woman came to the edge of the hayloft, pitchfork in hand and an anxious expression on her face as she looked down at Longarm.

He grinned and brushed off a few small pieces of straw that had settled on his coat. "Don't worry, ma'am, I'm fine," he told her.

"I didn't know anybody was around, or I wouldn't have thrown that hay down there."

"I reckon there are worse things around a stable that an hombre could have flung at him."

She laughed. "That's the truth. Hold on, and I'll come down." She tossed the pitchfork aside and went to a ladder at the edge of the hayloft.

Longarm hooked his thumbs in his vest pockets and watched with appreciation as Elizabeth Townsend climbed down the ladder. From where he was, he had a good view of muscular calves and thighs and that rounded rear end in tightly hugging denim. When she reached the ground, she turned to face him with a smile and asked, "What can I do for you?"

"You're Miss Townsend?"

"That's right."

"Sheriff Willard told me to come see you. I need to rent a good saddle mount, or buy one if you don't have any for rent."

"I think we can make arrangements for you to rent a horse, mister . . . ?"

"Long, Custis Long," he said, not mentioning that he was a deputy U.S. marshal. Willard could be trusted to keep that bit of information under his hat for the time being. In most cases, Longarm found that it was better to begin his assignments by not telling anyone he was a lawman unless he had to.

25

Elizabeth held out a hand. "Pleased to meet you, Mr. Long. I'm Elizabeth Townsend."

She was petite, not much over five feet tall, and she didn't look like the sort who could run a livery stable by herself. When Willard had first mentioned her, Longarm had imagined some big ol' horse-faced gal, and he realized now that he had jumped to a totally unfair conclusion. As he shook hands with her, he felt the strength in her grip, and he liked the way she looked him right in the eye, too. Despite her size and her undeniable beauty, Elizabeth Townsend was no frail hothouse flower. Of course, that sort of woman never lasted long in the West, anyway.

Longarm probably held on to her hand a little longer than he should have, but if she noticed, she gave no sign of it. Instead, she inclined her head toward the open door in the rear of the barn and said, "Come on out back. I've got some good saddle mounts in the corral."

He followed her outside. She put a booted foot on the bottom fence pole of a good-sized corral and rested crossed arms on one of the higher poles. "How about that sorrel?" she asked, indicating the animal she meant with a nod of her head.

Longarm put a foot on the fence, too, imitating her pose not in a mocking manner but more in a companionable way. After looking at the horse in question for a moment, he shook his head. "I don't think so. He looks like he'd be plenty fast, but he seems a mite high-strung to me."

Elizabeth glanced over at him and nodded. "You've got a good eye, Mr. Long. Tell me what you're most looking for. Speed, stamina, strength?"

"Something that'll do all right in the *Llano Caliente*."

Again she looked at him, but this time there was surprise in her expression. "The *Llano Caliente*?" she repeated. "You're going out there?"

"Probably. I ain't sure yet, but I don't hardly see how I can get out of it."

It was obvious that Elizabeth was quite curious about what sort of errand might take him out into the infamous desert. But she didn't ask questions, and after a moment, she pointed to a rawboned, mouse-colored horse with a darker stripe down its back. "That lineback dun is the one you want," she said. "They call them the breed that never quits."

Longarm nodded. "A captain I knew during the war had one like that he was sold on, and I've ridden quite a few of them myself. I'll have to fork a saddle to be sure, but I reckon he'll probably do."

"You need to rent a saddle and tack, too?"

"Just the tack. I've got a saddle. Left it over at the sheriff's office for now, but I'll go fetch it."

"All right. I'll bring the dun up front and get him ready."

Within the next quarter-hour, Longarm had slapped his McClellan saddle on the dun and ridden up and down along the street. He was more than satisfied with the horse, and when he drew rein in front of the livery stable, he nodded to Elizabeth.

"This is a fine mount," he admitted. "Let's get down to business."

She named a price, and he went into the office with her to pay it, leaving the dun tied up at a hitch rack in front of the barn. "It's a pleasure doing business with you, Mr. Long," she said as she handed him a receipt. "Do you plan to be in Castleton for a while?"

Longarm glanced at the afternoon light. He might take a ride over to the edge of the desert, but it was much too late in the day to venture out there. Besides, before he tried the *Llano Caliente*, he needed to round up some supplies, including some food, but mostly water and extra ammunition for the Winchester and the Colt. He said, "I reckon I'll be getting a hotel room, at least for tonight."

"Maybe I'll see you there," Elizabeth said. "I pick up

27

meals in their dining room for my father and myself."
Longarm quirked an eyebrow in surprise, and she
laughed. "I'm afraid I'm not much of a cook, Mr. Long.
I can handle a rope and a bridle better than most, but the
Good Lord didn't see fit to bless me overmuch with what
most people consider the feminine skills."

"I have trouble believing that, ma'am."

"You've never tried to eat anything I cooked."

"Well, then," Longarm said, "in that case, why don't
we plan on having dinner together at the hotel? Since
you'll be there anyway, you said."

He extended the invitation on an impulse, because he
felt a natural liking for Elizabeth Townsend. Not only
that, he told himself, but also she had been around this
area for a while, and he might be able to get some useful
information from her. He would question her carefully, so
that she wouldn't realize she was talking to a lawman.

And of course, she was damned pretty, and Longarm
wasn't in the habit of lying to himself. That was the main
reason he'd asked her to have dinner with him.

Elizabeth hesitated before answering, but finally she
nodded and said, "I suppose that would be all right. You'll
have to tell me, though, why you want to go out into the
awful desert."

Now that could prove to be a problem, thought Longarm, if he wanted to keep his real identity a secret for a
while. But he would think of something to tell her, he
decided. He said, "Seven o'clock?"

"I'll see you there," she promised. "I'll pick up Dad's
meal and bring it to him earlier, so I won't have to hurry."

That sounded good to Longarm. He tugged on the brim
of his hat, swung up onto the dun, and rode out of town
without looking back at Elizabeth Townsend.

He was regarding their dinner engagement with antic-
ipation, but that was still a ways off. Right now, he had
work to do.

Rampart Valley was about twenty miles wide, and Castleton was located near the center of it. That meant Longarm had a ten-mile ride to reach the edge of the *Llano Caliente*. Later, he would find out from Sheriff Willard exactly where the stolen cattle had entered the desert, but today, he just wanted to get a feel for the place.

As he rode through the valley on the dun, Longarm saw that it was indeed good cattle country, with shallow, rolling hills thickly carpeted with grass, wide meadows, and abundant creeks lined with stately cottonwood trees. Barbed wire fences, which had made inroads in other parts of the West, had not reached this part of the country yet, so he was able to ride freely without having to worry about barriers. He passed quite a few cattle, and a check of the brands told him that several different spreads ran their stock in the valley. Willard hadn't said anything about any trouble between the ranchers hereabouts, so Longarm assumed they all got along all right. Rampart Valley seemed pretty close to being idyllic—or it would have, if not for the rustlers that had begun plaguing the cattle shipments.

As Longarm rode west, the vegetation became more sparse, but not enough so as to prepare him for what he saw as he topped a rise. A couple of hundred yards away at the bottom of the slope, the grassland stopped and the desert began. The dividing line was almost as sharp as if someone had drawn the tip of a gigantic pencil across the landscape and decreed that no more grass would grow west of that point. Instead, there were only gently undulating sand dunes as far as the eye could see, shining in the late afternoon sunlight, dotted here and there by scrubby mesquite bushes too small to be called trees, even though that's what they really were.

Longarm reined the dun to a stop and leaned forward in the saddle, a frown on his face as he studied the arid

29

terrain spread out in front of him. He wasn't sure what freak of nature was responsible for the formation of the *Llano Caliente*, but it had done a good job of making the desert unlivable. The presence of the mesquites meant there was some water in the ground, but more than likely it was far beneath the surface. Longarm knew it was common for a tiny desert bush to have roots thirty or forty, even ninety, feet long. The stubborn foliage would thrust its roots as deep as it had to in order to obtain moisture.

But farther into the desert, it was unlikely that even the hardy mesquites could survive. A herd of thirsty cows sure as hell couldn't, not if it hoped to make a drive of at least forty miles. Anybody fool enough to attempt that would end up with nothing but a trail of skeletons stretched across the sands.

So where had the rustled stock gone? Longarm couldn't answer that question just yet. It was possible the rustlers had driven the cattle into the desert a short distance, then turned around and come out again at a different place. He would have to ask Willard if the sheriff had ever thought to check for tracks *leaving* the desert. If Willard hadn't covered that possibility, Longarm's first move probably would be to check it out himself.

He turned and rode back toward Castleton, convinced that there had to be an explanation. He had seen plenty of odd things during his long career as a star packer for the Justice Department, things that appeared to have no rational explanation, but every time he had found the answer to the puzzle and brought the lawbreakers to justice. He didn't intend for that record to be ruined here in Rampart Valley.

It was nearly sunset when he reached Castleton. When he rode into the livery stable, Elizabeth wasn't there. Instead, an old man came out of the tack room to take the dun. For a second, Longarm wondered if the man was Elizabeth's father, but then he remembered that the elder

Townsend was supposed to be an invalid of some sort.

"Howdy," the old-timer greeted Longarm. He was bald except for a fringe of white hair around his ears and had a high-pitched voice. "Lizzie told me somebody rented that dun. Name's Alf."

"Glad to meet you, Alf," Longarm said as he swung down from the saddle and handed the reins to the old man. "You work here?"

"Damned straight. I been the hostler for as long as the stable's been here. Worked for old Tom Townsend for many a year, and now I work for his gal." Alf jerked a thumb over his shoulder. "Dun'll be in the second stall on the right, case you want it while nobody's around. When we got a hoss rented, we keep it in here instead of out in the corral, so folks can get to it easier."

"Makes sense," Longarm said with a nod. "I guess Miss Townsend's gone to fetch supper for her pa?"

"Yep, and then she's supposed to eat supper with some fella. Must really think a heap of him, too, 'cause I heard her sayin' somethin' about takin' a bath." Alf gave Longarm a sudden sharp glance. "Say, you wouldn't be the fella, would you?"

"Could be," Longarm allowed with a grin.

"Well, then, I been talkin' out of school. Just never you mind 'bout anything I said. I reckon Lizzie wouldn't go an' take a bath on account of the likes of you."

Longarm chuckled. "Probably not."

He left the dun at the stable and walked down the street to the hotel. He should have gotten a room earlier, he told himself, but he'd been anxious to have a look at the *Llano Caliente*. If the hotel was full up, he might be in a fix. Surely there would be somewhere else in town he could stay, he thought.

Luck was with Longarm. The clerk at the desk had a room for him. Second floor rear. Longarm paid for it, got the key, and then walked across the street to the sheriff's office. Willard wasn't there, but Longarm's warbag and Winchester were, stashed behind the desk where Longarm had left them. He picked them up and went back to the hotel, but instead of going through the lobby and up the main stairs, he walked along the alley beside the building to an outside staircase he'd noticed. Since his room was in the rear, it would be easy to get there by using those stairs.

The warbag was in his left hand, the Winchester tucked under the same arm. He went up the stairs to the small landing and opened the door there. As he stepped inside, he caught a glimpse of one of the doors that lined both sides of the hallway swinging shut. Pausing, Longarm looked at the key he fished out of his pocket. It had a paper tag attached to it, and the number 17 was scrawled in pencil on the tag. The light in the corridor was pretty dim, but he thought the number on the door he had just seen closing was 17.

Well, now, that was mighty interesting, he thought. He had just rented that room. There shouldn't have been anyone inside it.

Unless whoever it was, was waiting for him.

Silently, Longarm set the warbag on the floor of the hall and eased the outside door closed behind him. He took the Winchester in both hands as he started along the hall toward Room 17. For a big man, he moved very quietly. His breathing was under control, his mind was clear, and his senses were all on the alert. As he paused in front of the door, he caught a faint whiff of bay rum and tobacco lingering in the air.

The possibility that it could be Elizabeth waiting in his room had crossed his mind. She hadn't seemed the type to be so bold and brazen, and Longarm prided himself on being a pretty good judge of women, but anything was possible. No matter what, though, he couldn't imagine

32

that she would be wearing bay rum. She probably didn't smoke, either.

No, that was a gent in his room, Longarm decided, and he couldn't figure out who it might be since he didn't know anybody in Castleton except Sheriff Willard and old Alf down at the livery stable. Alf was out, because Longarm had just left him at the stable. He supposed his visitor could be Willard. If the sheriff had come in and asked, the clerk downstairs likely would have told him which room the stranger called Long had just rented.

So with that possibility in mind, Longarm knew he couldn't go in shooting. He would have to wait to see what happened—and that meant that if his visitor did intend to bushwhack him, the son of a bitch would be able to get in the first shot.

Longarm would just have to make sure that shot missed.

He reached out, grasped the knob, and turned it slowly and silently until the knob was open but the door was still pulled shut. Then he gave it a sudden shove and threw himself forward, landing on the carpet runner and rolling across the open doorway. He brought the barrel of the Winchester up.

Flame lanced from inside the darkened room. Longarm fired the rifle and levered another round into the chamber as he kept rolling. His second shot came hard on the heels of the first. Then he was past the door but not safe yet. Far from it if the gunman inside the room wanted to keep the fight going. The hotel's interior walls were thin enough that they wouldn't stop a bullet. The man could blast away right through the wall at Longarm.

No more shots came from inside the room, however. Instead Longarm heard the crash of broken glass. The bastard was going out through the window. Longarm came up on his knees, brought the Winchester to his shoulder, and fired three times as fast as he could work the rifle's lever. The .44-40 slugs punched through the wall, leaving neat holes behind. Longarm surged to his feet and darted to the door, throwing himself through it in a hurry so that he wouldn't be silhouetted against the light in the hall for any longer than he had to be.

Ducking to the right, Longarm pivoted, tracking the barrel of the Winchester around the room. Nothing moved. No more shots sounded. Longarm saw the curtains fluttering over the broken window. In the glow from the lamp at the end of the hall, he saw a small table with a kerosene lamp sitting on it. He held the Winchester ready in his right hand while he used the left to find a match, strike it, and light the lamp.

The room was empty, he saw as a yellow glow spread from the wick. He lowered the lamp's chimney and the light grew even stronger. It showed him a few pieces of glass scattered on the floor underneath the window, but he figured most of the broken glass had fallen in the alley outside, since the window had been smashed outward by the escaping intruder. He moved closer to the window and used the barrel of the rifle to move the curtains aside. The bushwhacker had shattered all four panes of glass when he busted out. Longarm looked for blood, but didn't see any. That meant none of his shots had found their target, and also that the bushwhacker hadn't cut himself on the glass, at least not badly. That was a damned shame.

Longarm became aware of yelling elsewhere in the hotel. Probably everybody in the place had heard those gunshots and started bellowing for help. It came as no surprise a couple of minutes later when he heard heavy footsteps approaching fast in the hall outside.

Sheriff Stan Willard appeared in the open doorway of the room, carrying a shotgun. When his startled gaze fell on Longarm, who was standing carefully to one side of the busted window, he exclaimed, "What the hell happened here?"

"A misunderstanding, I reckon," Longarm said.

"A misunderstanding with bullets?"

"Somebody was waiting inside my room," Longarm said. "Either he had a grudge against somebody in the hotel and waited in the wrong room, or else he was trying to rob me." The clerk and some of the other guests were peering curiously over Willard's shoulder by now. "Either way, it was a mistake. I'm just a stranger passing through, Sheriff, and I don't have enough money to make it worth anybody's time to rob me."

A light dawned in Willard's eyes, and Longarm knew the sheriff had picked up the hint. He didn't want Willard to blurt out the fact that he was really a deputy marshal.

"I'm mighty sorry, mister," Willard said. "Normally, Castleton is a mighty peaceable town."

"I'd like to believe you, Sheriff," Longarm said, "but after this . . ."

The clerk spoke up. "Of course, the hotel will refund the cost of your night's stay, Mr. Long. And we'll put you up in another room."

"That's mighty decent of you, old son, but I still don't like people shooting at me."

"Where did the bushwhacker go?" Willard asked. "I don't see him still in here."

"Out the window," Longarm said, gesturing at the broken panes with the rifle.

Willard came over and peered out the window. He clucked his tongue and shook his head. "I was sort of hoping the son of a bitch would be lying down in the alley with a busted leg. No such luck, though. There's a closed-up rain barrel down there. He must've dropped on top of it and then jumped the rest of the way into the alley. It wouldn't have been more than a five foot drop to that barrel."

"I'd lay odds that's what happened," Longarm agreed.

"I'll look into it, Mr . . . Long, was it? I don't like trouble in my town. I'll find out who was responsible for this."

"I hope you do, Sheriff," Longarm said, but he wasn't convinced it was going to happen. Whoever the bushwhacker was, he had gotten away in a pretty smooth fashion.

Now there were more troubling questions to plague his mind, Longarm thought. The explanations he had offered Willard *could* be true, but Longarm didn't believe for a minute that they were. Any time a lawman rode into a town and had an attempt made on his life that same day, chances were the shooting was connected to the case that had brought him here. The problem with that was that he hadn't told anyone in Castleton who he really was except Willard, and Longarm still trusted the local lawman. The bushwhacker must have found out his true identity some other way.

He would have to ponder that later. For now, he had something else to do.

"Where's that other room you're going to give me?" he asked the hotel clerk as he went out into the hall and picked up his warbag. "I've got a dinner engagement, and I don't want the young lady to have to wait."

Chapter 4

The hotel clerk took Longarm to another room while Sheriff Willard poked around the room where the shoot-out had taken place, looking for clues to the bush-whacker's identity. Longarm knew the sheriff wouldn't find any—he had already searched the room thoroughly himself—but he didn't try to discourage Willard.

Once he was settled into the other room, he washed up using a pitcher of water and a basin that sat on a small table, and then he put on a clean shirt. He shrugged into his vest, buttoning it and adjusting the chain that ran across his chest from one pocket to the other. At one end of the chain was the heavy silver pocket watch he carried; at the other, acting as a watch fob of sorts, was a two-shot .41 caliber derringer. The chain was welded to the frame of the little gun. As a hideout weapon, it had saved Longarm's bacon more times than he liked to count.

He tied his ribbon tie, put on his coat, and settled the snuff brown Stetson on his head. He looked respectable enough, he decided after glancing in the mirror. Lemon-ade Lucy, the wife of President Rutherford B. Hayes, had prevailed upon her husband to make it standard procedure for all government employees to dress nicely, in suits if possible. Longarm didn't resent the First Lady for that decision, as long as he didn't have to wear the brown tweeds when he was riding the range. So far, the regulation hadn't been extended to that point. If the day ever came when it was, Longarm knew he might have to give some thought to changing his line of work. But after all these years, what in the world would he do with himself if he weren't a lawman anymore? He had done some cowboying as a young man, but he was too old for that now. Too set in his ways, as well.

He put those thoughts out of his mind. No point in worrying about the future, he told himself, when he had a full plate here in the present. Not only did he have a case to solve and a gang of cattle and mail thieves to chase down, but he had Elizabeth Townsend waiting for him in the dining room downstairs, too. He checked his watch as he left the room. Only a few minutes after seven. Maybe Elizabeth wasn't getting too impatient.

She didn't seem upset when he came into the dining room a couple of minutes later. She was sitting at one of the tables with a smile on her face, toying with the stem of the glass of wine in front of her. Longarm wouldn't have expected anybody to be drinking wine in a cowtown like Castleton, especially not a gal who ran a livery stable, but he reminded himself that Elizabeth was full of surprises. Likely it would pay him to quit jumping to conclusions about her.

She looked up at him as he approached the table, and her smile widened. "Hello, Mr. Long," she said, her voice soft and musical.

"Call me Custis," he requested as he took off his hat and laid it on the table. "You look mighty pretty this evening, Miss Townsend."

That was the truth. Elizabeth wore a light blue gown that left most of her shoulders bare and swooped low in the front. Some white lace attached to the bodice of the dress concealed the valley between her breasts, but there were enough openings in the lace to give a tantalizing hint of the smooth, creamy flesh underneath it. The gown wasn't all that fancy, but again, for a place like Castleton, it was fairly elegant.

"If I'm going to call you Custis, you have to call me Elizabeth," she said.

Longarm pulled back the chair opposite her, sat down, and smiled. "I reckon I can do that, all right."

"I hope you don't mind that I took the liberty of having the waiter bring a bottle of wine."

Longarm shook his head. "Nope." A second glass had been poured already. He picked it up and sipped the rich red liquid. He was no expert on wine, being more of a Maryland rye man himself, but the stuff was good, with just enough bite to create a pleasant glow inside his belly.

The waiter approached the table, and Longarm nodded to let him know it was all right. "You've eaten here and I haven't," he said to Elizabeth. "What do you reckon we should order?"

"The baked chicken is very good."

Longarm nodded again. Given his druthers, he might have preferred a thick, juicy steak, rare enough he'd have to stab it to keep it from running off, but if Elizabeth wanted chicken, that was all right with him. He ordered the baked chicken with all the trimmings for both of them and then sat back to sip his wine and enjoy looking across the table at Elizabeth. He was able to put completely out of his mind the fact that less than an hour earlier, some son of a bitch hiding in his room had tried to let daylight through him.

While they were waiting for their food, Longarm steered the conversation around to Elizabeth's life here in Castleton, thinking that he could find out some background on the town in that fashion. And he was genuinely interested in learning more about her, too. She explained that her father, Tom Townsend, had moved to Castleton just before the Civil War, not long after the town was founded, bringing along his pregnant wife Judith.

"So you were born here?" Longarm asked.

Elizabeth nodded. "That's right."

"Any brothers or sisters?"

"No. I was their first child, and my mother died giving birth to me."

"Oh," Longarm said. "I'm sorry."

"That's all right," Elizabeth told him. "Needless to say, I never knew her except from looking at a few photographs my father has. He says that she was a fine woman, though, and that's good enough for me."

"Of course it is." Longarm paused. "So your pa raised you by himself?"

"That's right. I grew up in the stable. I suppose it was inevitable that I would be a tomboy."

Longarm smiled across the table at her. "Begging your pardon, Elizabeth, but you sure don't look like no tomboy tonight."

"Thank you, Custis," she said, returning his smile, and he could tell that she was pleased by the compliment. "A few of the ladies here in town have taken me under their wing, so to speak, and made me their . . . project, I guess you could say. They've tried to teach me how to dress and act like a lady. I don't think they've been too successful so far, though. I'm still more comfortable in jeans, with a lariat or a pitchfork in my hand."

"Nothing wrong with that. You're earning an honest living and taking care of your pa. What's wrong with him, if you don't mind me asking?"

An expression of sadness crept over Elizabeth's face, and Longarm regretted posing the question. She didn't hesitate in answering it, though. "He had some sort of seizure about a year ago. After that, he couldn't use his legs anymore, and his right arm doesn't work properly, either."

"Must be hard on you, taking care of him."

"It's harder on him," Elizabeth said. "After working for all those years, to suddenly be unable to do almost everything . . . well, I don't mind telling you I was afraid he might just give up and . . . will himself to die. But he hasn't. He always wants to hear everything about what's going on at the stable. He tries to keep up with what's happening in town, too."

"You must have to spend a lot of time with him."

"Some. Alf helps out. You probably met him . . . ?"

Longarm nodded. "When I brought the dun back."

"And the ladies from the Baptist Church come over and help out, too. We manage. Sometimes it's not easy . . ." Elizabeth shrugged. "But life hardly ever is, is it?"

"I reckon not," Longarm agreed. He changed the subject. "Being in the livery business, I'll bet you know just about everybody around these parts."

"I suppose I do."

"What about the ranchers here in the valley?"

"Of course. Most of them have owned their spreads ever since I was a little girl."

"Any of them what you'd consider a troublemaker?"

Elizabeth frowned, clearly confused by the question. "Not at all. We've never had any range wars or anything like that around here. Why would you ask such a thing?" Before he could answer, she went on, "Just what brings you to Castleton anyway, Custis?"

The arrival of the waiter with the food saved Longarm from having to answer that question right away, but he could tell by the look on her face that she wasn't going to forget about it. He had aroused her curiosity, and he would have to satisfy it before she would let go. He could tell she had a stubborn streak and didn't mind indulging it.

String beans, baked potatoes, and biscuits with honey and butter accompanied the chicken. The food was good, Longarm discovered as he dug into the meal, and he enjoyed it, washing it down with the wine. It seemed like he recalled some rule about how you weren't supposed to drink red wine with chicken, but he didn't know who had come up with that and didn't care. Good was good, and to hell with the rules.

He was buttering another biscuit when Elizabeth said, "You were about to tell me what brings you to Castleton, Custis."

Longarm lowered his voice to a conspiratorial tone and said, "All right, but you've got to promise to keep it under your bonnet."

Elizabeth nodded. "I promise."

"I work for a land and cattle syndicate back East," Longarm said. "They're thinking about expanding their holdings into Rampart Valley, and my job's to look around and let them know how things stack up around here." He had thought about it, and while he hated lying to Elizabeth, the story he had just told her would give him an excuse for riding around the valley and poking his nose in wherever he wanted to.

She gave him a dubious frown and said, "All the best land in the valley is claimed and has been for years. The ranches are well-established."

"Maybe some of the cattlemen hereabouts would be interested in selling their spreads."

Elizabeth shook her head. "I wouldn't count on that, Custis. You know how these old-timers are. Once they put down roots, it's hard to budge them. I mean, I know you have to do your job, but I don't think you're going to be very successful."

"Maybe not. Could be that once I deliver my report, my bosses will decide to look elsewhere."

"I really think that would be their best course of action.

Some of the ranchers . . . well, they're a little crusty. They won't even like being asked if they want to sell out."

"I'll be careful," Longarm promised.

The explanation seemed to satisfy Elizabeth. She didn't say anything else about the matter as they finished their meal with dishes of cherry cobbler. When Longarm remarked on how good the cobbler was, Elizabeth said, "The cherries were grown right here in the valley, you know. Several of the ranchers have fruit orchards as well."

"Sounds like Rampart Valley is pretty close to being heaven on earth," Longarm said.

"I'm sure it has its flaws, but I've never wanted to live anywhere else."

When they were done eating, Longarm stood up and held Elizabeth's chair for her. "It was a mighty nice evening," he told her. "I'd be honored to walk you home." He would have liked to take her upstairs to his room, but he wasn't going to suggest that. Despite her self-disparaging remarks about lariats and pitchforks, Elizabeth was a lady, and Longarm didn't want to offend her with a blatant suggestion of a little slap-and-tickle session. Now, if she came up with the idea on her own . . .

"Thank you," she said. She picked up a lace shawl from the table, and he draped it around her shoulders. No matter how hot it got during the day, at this high altitude the air always cooled off rapidly once the sun went down.

Longarm kept his eyes open as he walked down the street beside her. An attempt had been made on his life tonight, and the bushwhacker had gotten away. It was possible the hombre would try again, and Longarm didn't want Elizabeth getting in the way of a bullet meant for him. He probably shouldn't have offered to walk her home, he told himself, but he'd made the offer out of habit before he thought things through.

"My father and I have a little house behind the stable,"

she told him when he asked where she lived. "It's always been home."

Longarm took out a cheroot and chewed it without lighting it. "I reckon it must be nice to have a place like that, where you've always been comfortable."

"You never had a real home?"

"I was born and raised in West-by-God Virginia, but I didn't stay there very long once I came of age. There was a war on, and I had a hankering to join up."

"You fought in the Civil War?"

Longarm grinned around the cheroot. "Yeah, but don't ask me on which side. I sort of disremember."

"I understand," Elizabeth said with a little laugh. "That was a long time ago, and we're all Americans again now."

"Yep, that's the way I look at it. Anyway, when that was over, I got fiddle-footed again and moseyed on out here to the frontier."

"You never settled down anywhere?"

"The, ah, syndicate I work for has an office in Denver, and I keep a rented room there. But they send me all over, from the Milk River to the Rio Grande and the Mississippi to the Pacific Ocean." To tell the truth, his job had taken him even farther than those wide-flung boundaries, but he didn't go into that. "I reckon I've seen just about every place there is to see."

Elizabeth sighed. "There's a part of me that wishes I could say that. It's odd, isn't it? When you talk about having a home like I do, I can hear something in your voice that says you've always missed that. But I've been here in Castleton all my life, and sometimes I wish I could go somewhere else—anywhere else!—just to get out of here. I guess there really is some truth to that old saying about the grass being greener on the other side of the fence."

"You know why that is, don't you?" asked Longarm.

"No, why?"

"There's more manure over there," he said.

Elizabeth looked up at him for a second and then burst out laughing. "I suppose that must be true," she said as she took his arm. He enjoyed the warmth of her fingers that came through his jacket and shirtsleeves.

A moment later, she said, "I really ought to look in at the stable before I go on home, if you don't mind."

"Nope. Alf's not there?"

"No, he's with my father. They play checkers nearly every night after Alf has tended to the horses. He has a bunk in the tack room, but he won't turn in until after I've gotten home."

The double doors on the front of the barn were closed for the night. Elizabeth led the way to a smaller door that opened into the office. She went in first, moving with the ease of long practice despite the darkness, and lit a lamp. Longarm shut the door, not wanting to present too tempting a target if some gunman was trailing them. He didn't think that was the case, but he had lived as long as he had by being careful.

Elizabeth picked up the lamp from the desk and walked out into the barn, moving down the center aisle to check on the horses in the stalls. Longarm leaned a shoulder against one of the posts holding up the roof and watched her. She stopped to speak softly to several of the horses, and when she reached over the gates that closed off the stalls, the horses nuzzled her hand with obvious affection. Longarm smiled as she turned and came back toward him.

"What?" she asked, noticing his expression.

"It appears those horses are right fond of you."

"I'm fond of them, too. A good horse is a wonderful creature, one of God's finest gifts to man."

Longarm had never thought of them in such high-flown terms, but he nodded. "I reckon you're probably right."

Elizabeth carried the lamp into the office and set it down on the desk, but she didn't blow out the flame.

Instead she turned back to Longarm and said, "As much as I like horses, though, they can't take the place of other things." She moved closer to Longarm and put a hand on his arm. "A horse can't put his arms around you and hold you."

"No," said Longarm, "I reckon he can't." She was close enough so that he could smell the fresh fragrance of her hair.

"Custis, I . . . I would really like it if you would hold me right now."

"Elizabeth," he murmured, "I'd be glad to oblige."

He slid his arms around her and drew her against him. With a sigh, she rested her head against his broad chest. He felt a tiny tremble go through her. She whispered, "That feels so good."

He kept one hand in the small of her back and reached up to stroke her hair with the other. "You stay here just as long as you want," he told her and meant it. He could feel the soft prod of her breasts against him, and her warmth and nearness were exciting him, no doubt about that. But he could wait until she was good and ready for more, and if that didn't happen, well, he could live with that, too.

After a few minutes, she said, "You're a very kind, generous man."

Longarm chuckled. "Most folks say I'm rough as a cob."

She lifted her head so that she could look up into his face. "Oh, no! I could tell as soon as I saw you that you were a gentleman."

"Figured that out from how I jumped out of the way of that hay you were throwing at me, did you?"

She laughed and said, "That was an accident." Her face grew more solemn as she went on, "This isn't. I'm throwing myself at you now, Custis, and I'm doing it on purpose. I want you to kiss me."

46

Once again, Longarm was glad to oblige.

Her mouth was hot and wet and sweet, and Longarm thoroughly enjoyed the taste of it. Her lips parted and her tongue explored boldly. He met it with his own, and they darted and swirled around each other in a sensuous dance. His hand moved down from the small of her back to the swell of her hips. He caressed her bottom, finding it as taut and rounded as it had looked in her denim jeans earlier that day. She pressed against him, and as his shaft grew hard she could not have missed its insistent prodding against the softness of her belly. Her hands clutched at his jacket, and as he felt the growing urgency with which she molded herself to him, he knew he wouldn't have to worry about stopping. She wanted this every bit as much as he did, needed it perhaps even more.

She broke the passionate kiss and whispered, "The loft . . . ! There's a blanket up there . . ."

That sounded like a mighty fine idea to Longarm.

Moments later, they were climbing the ladder to the hayloft, Elizabeth going up first, Longarm right behind her so that he had to resist the temptation to rest his face against the cushions of her rump. He didn't want to startle her and make her lose her grip on the rungs. That would be a hell of a note, if they both fell off the ladder right now.

It was dark in the loft, only a faint glow from the lamp in the office penetrating up here. But there was enough light for Longarm to see Elizabeth's fingers going to the buttons of her dress. He took off his hat and coat and boots while she was peeling down to her shift. Then she came over to him and said, "Take off your gunbelt and let me do the rest of it. It's been too long since I undressed a man."

Considering her age, Longarm didn't figure she had undressed too many men in her life, but clearly she had some experience. He unbuckled the gunbelt, coiled it up, and set it and the holstered Colt aside. Elizabeth unbuttoned his vest and took it off of him, hesitating a little when she felt the weight of the derringer. She must have thought it was just a watch, though, because she set it aside without comment. Then she used her teeth to pull on one side of his tie, surprising a pleased laugh out of him. Former tomboy or not, Elizabeth Townsend was one hell of a woman.

She took his shirt off him and ran her fingers through the thick mat of hair on his chest. At the same time, he fondled her breasts through her shift, feeling the hardness of her nipples against the soft fabric. She reached down to his trousers, fumbled a little with the buttons, but got them open. She reached inside his long underwear and closed her fingers around his manhood.

"Oh," she breathed. "Oh, that feels so nice."

What she was doing felt pretty damned good to Longarm, too. She continued stroking him with one hand while she used the other to push down his underwear and trousers. He managed to step out of them, then he hooked his thumbs under the shoulder straps of her shift and eased them off her shoulders. The flimsy garment fell around her hips. Longarm slid it the rest of the way off of her.

"I'd better . . . get that blanket," she said, clearly having trouble catching her breath now. Longarm nodded. He was starting to feel a mite breathless himself.

Elizabeth turned away, her sleek, pale body gleaming in the faint light. She took the blanket down from a hook where it hung on the wall, shook it out, and then spread it over a pile of hay.

"It may be a little rough," she apologized.

"I don't reckon I'll mind too much if you don't," Longarm told her.

She lay down on the blanket and spread her legs, opening herself to him. He could see the dark triangle at the juncture of her thighs. "We can do all sorts of things later," she said, "but right now I need you inside me, Custis. Please, don't make me wait."

Longarm dropped to a crouch, positioning himself over her. His shaft was so hard it ached with every throb of heated blood through it, and he knew there was only one way to relieve that tension. As he knelt between Elizabeth's widespread legs, he reached out and found the folds of her femininity. They were already drenched with moisture, telling him she was more than ready for his penetration. His thumb brushed the little bud of flesh at the top of her gateway, and the touch made her gasp. She gave a little moan and whispered, "Now, Custis, now."

He brought the head of his shaft to her opening and began to slide into her. Inch by inch, he insinuated the long, thick pole of male flesh inside her. She helped him along with little jerks of her hips. Finally, after what seemed like a maddeningly long time, his entire shaft was imbedded within her. He let enough of his weight down on her so that he felt her breasts flatten against his chest. Lowering his head, he kissed her again. Her arms went around his neck, and her legs encircled his hips. She crossed her ankles and began to pump her hips. Longarm fell right into the sensuous rhythm with her.

It was the simplest thing in the world, yet infinitely complicated, always similar, yet never exactly the same. Longarm surged in and out of her for long moments, making waves of pure pleasure wash over both of them. There was nothing better, nothing that mattered more at this particular moment in time, this specific place in the universe. Longarm thrust harder into her, reaching greater depths, and Elizabeth's arms and legs tightened around him with incredible strength, as if to pull him still deeper inside her. He felt his climax boiling up and was glad when she cried out against his mouth, because he knew that her culmination was sweeping over her, too. He shuddered and emptied himself inside her.

When Longarm was finished, Elizabeth gave a great, trembling sigh. "I hoped," she whispered. "I hoped, but I never dreamed . . . Custis, you sweet, sweet man . . ."

Longarm held her, not rolling off until his now-flaccid organ finally shrank to the point that it slipped out of her. Even then, he kept his arms around her and brought her with him as he rolled onto his side.

"I'm so glad you came to Castleton," she said.

"So am I," he told her as he snuggled her against him.

He just hoped they could both still say the same when the case that had brought him here was over.

Chapter 5

Dressed in denim trousers and jacket and butternut shirt, Longarm rode along the border between Rampart Valley and the *Llano Caliente* the next day, his keen eyes searching the ground for any sign of cattle leaving the desert. Early this morning, he had slipped into Sheriff Willard's office and discussed with the lawman the possibility that the rustlers hadn't gone across the desert at all but had turned the stolen herds around and emerged from the sands at a different point.

"I hadn't thought of that," Willard admitted. Coffee was brewing on the cast-iron stove but wasn't ready yet. "That would sure explain where those damned cows got off to. You see, Marshal, it takes a fella like you to think of such a thing."

Longarm grinned. "You mean I think like a rustler?"

"Sometimes the only way to catch an owlhoot is to figure out what's goin' on inside his head."

Longarm nodded in agreement. He had found that to be true in his own years of packing a badge.

"Say," Willard commented, "did you get yourself a good horse from Townsend's Livery?"

"I think so," Longarm replied. "Reckon I'll find out

more about it today, because I plan to do quite a bit of riding."

"Heard that you had supper last night in the hotel dining room with Elizabeth Townsend. You know, that gal's almost like a daughter to me. Her pa and me been friends for nigh on to twenty years."

"She seems mighty nice, all right," Longarm said.

Willard fiddled with the coffeepot. "Sure wouldn't want to see her get hurt," he said without looking at Longarm.

Longarm swallowed the irritation he felt welling up inside him. Willard was the one who'd sent him to the stable in the first place. The sheriff had no call to go and get all protective now.

Of course, Willard had suggested that Longarm could rent a horse there, not seduce the gal who ran the place. Come to think of it, though, there hadn't been much seduction involved, and what there was had originated as much from Elizabeth as from him.

Now, as he rode along with the desert on his right and the valley on his left, heading south, he tried to put all that out of his mind. He had a job to do. That was the only real reason he was here.

On a map of the valley pinned to the wall of the sheriff's office, Willard had shown him the places where the eastbound trains had been stopped, as well as roughly tracing the paths taken by the stolen herds as they were driven toward the desert. To Longarm's way of thinking, the sites of the holdups didn't matter much. They were all fairly close together, around blind curves so that the engineers hadn't been able to see the log barriers erected across the tracks in time to do anything other than bring their locomotives screeching to a stop. Once that was done, the members of the gang had come racing out of the nearby trees, some on foot and some mounted. They took over the trains and went about their business in a grimly efficient, almost silent manner, according to the witnesses. No one had been killed during the robberies, though a couple of express messengers and several cowboys accompanying the cattle had been wounded when they put up a fight.

After being unloaded from the train, the cattle had been driven cross-country toward the desert. Longarm had memorized the map in Willard's office and knew where each herd had entered the *Llano Caliente*. He found the places without much trouble and discovered that a few signs of the herds' passage remained, despite the amount of time that had gone by since then. Longarm's alertness increased. If he could still see where the cattle had gone into the desert, he ought to be able to see where they came out—*if* they came back out.

By midday, he was well past the southernmost spot where one of the herds had entered the sands. He hadn't found any indication that a herd had come back out. In fact, he hadn't found many tracks leading into and out of the desert at all. Cows weren't the smartest critters in the world, but even they had more sense than to wander out onto those burning sands unless they were forced to. Likewise, the other animals that lived in the valley avoided the desert. Longarm found a few tracks where rabbits had ventured a short distance onto the sand to gnaw at mesquite beans, but that was all.

He brought the dun to a halt, glared at the desert, and frowned in thought. His idea that the stolen herds hadn't crossed the desert but had turned around and come back out instead had been a good one, but it was becoming obvious to him that it was wrong. Driving the stolen cattle for miles and miles in a northsouth direction in the desert was just as unlikely as pushing them an equal distance west across the sands toward the Solomon Mountains.

That "thin air" comment of Willard's was starting to look more and more right, mused Longarm.

He knew better, though. Cattle didn't just disappear.

They went into the desert, and they had wound up somewhere else.

Unless, Longarm thought suddenly, they were still in there somewhere.

He grimaced, tugged at his earlobe, scraped a thumbnail along the line of his jaw. That was crazy. Who would steal cattle just to drive them into the desert and leave them there to die? No owlhoot would risk stopping a train and rustling those beeves in the first place unless there was some sort of payoff involved. Try as he might, Longarm couldn't think of any way anybody could make money by abandoning the cattle to die of thirst.

And there was no way they could still be alive in the middle of the desert . . . was there?

Now that the thought had entered his brain, it refused to stop nagging at him. Whether the idea made sense or not, it was the only answer that hadn't been checked out yet. And there was only one way to find out if it was true or not.

"Old son, I hope you don't mind the heat too much," Longarm said to the dun. "We're about to take us a ride into the *Llano Caliente*."

He thought about Elizabeth as he pushed on into the desert. She had been true to her word. After their first bout of lovemaking was over, they had lingered there on the blanket in the hayloft for hours, fondling and exploring each other's bodies with lips, tongues, and fingers. She had been especially excited by sprawling out on top of him with her head over his groin so that she could give him a proper French lesson while he was doing the same to her at the other end. He had used his thumbs to spread her nether lips wide and slid his tongue into her, making her hips jerk and bounce wildly. He had to hold on tight to keep her still enough for him to finish her off. About the same time, his shaft was erupting in her mouth, and she eagerly swallowed what he gave her. Later, when he had recovered, they had made love yet again, and when they were finished, Elizabeth had sighed and said, "What would the ladies from the church think if they could see me now?"

"Probably that you were wanton and shameless, and they'd wish they could be more like that themselves, more than likely."

Elizabeth had laughed and kissed him. "I'd like to think you're right, Custis. You know, you're the sweetest man I've ever met."

"Much obliged for the compliment, ma'am."

He was still a little worried that whoever had taken that shot at him in his hotel room had seen him with Elizabeth. The idea that her life might be in danger because of him nagged at him. He thought she ought to be all right there in Castleton, though, surrounded as she was by friends and acquaintances. From what Sheriff Willard had said about her, Longarm had the idea that he kept an eye on Elizabeth to start with. He would probably be even more diligent now.

As he rode deeper into the desert, Longarm's thoughts returned to the job at hand. As he had suspected, the mesquite trees became fewer and farther between, meaning that the sources of moisture were drying up, even deep beneath the shifting sands. There were low places, however, where several of the hardy plants clustered together. If a gent could dig deep enough, he might find water in those depressions.

A wind blew steadily, not hard, but enough to keep the sand moving. Longarm had heard sand dunes referred to as walking hills, because they never stayed in one place. Under the constant urging of the wind, the sand trickled here and there, changing the contours of the landscape. At night, when everything was quiet, you could hear the sand moving, whispering and murmuring to itself. It was a sound that had been known to drive greenhorns mad, because they became convinced that someone was out there in the darkness when, really, there was nothing but miles and miles of empty desert.

Looking for old tracks was futile. They vanished overnight. But around the middle of the afternoon, Longarm ran across a fresh sign. It was hard to tell from the marks left in the soft sand, but Longarm thought he was looking at the hoofprints of a couple of horses. Somebody was riding in the desert today besides him.

He reined in and frowned in thought. Before he'd made this discovery, he had been leaning toward turning around and heading back to Rampart Valley. The sun was blistering hot and his shirt was soaked with sweat. He had brought four full canteens with him, but two of them were empty now because he had stopped fairly often so that he and the dun could drink. He still had plenty of water to get back but not so much that he could afford to waste any. He leaned over and patted the dun's shoulder. The horse was lathered with sweat, too.

"What about it, old son?" he asked as if the dun could understand him. "Do we trail these rannies, or do we get out of this hellhole while we can? If we turn around and go back to Rampart Valley, these tracks will be long gone before we can get out here tomorrow."

The dun turned its head and looked at him, but no other answer came from the horse. Longarm chuckled.

"Let's go," he said, heeling the dun into a walk. He started following the tracks.

The mouse-colored horse was proving to be as good a mount as Longarm had expected. Despite the long hours they had spent on the trail already today, the dun was still strong, and Longarm pushed him fairly hard over the next hour as he followed the hoofprints. He stopped then, to rest the dun and to let both of them drink. While the horse stood there regaining some of its strength, Longarm climbed on foot to the top of a thirty-foot tall dune and peered to the west, using his hat to shade his eyes. He felt a sudden quickening of his pulse as he spotted a couple of dark specks moving against the light-colored sand.

Those specks were the riders he was following. He was sure of it.

He watched for a moment as the riders disappeared, then came into view again as they topped another dune. Gauging their pace, Longarm decided they were taking their time. That was the smart thing to do. Hurrying in the desert usually just meant that a fella died even quicker than he would have otherwise.

But the riders were no more than half a mile in front of him, which meant that Longarm could catch up if he didn't mind pushing his own mount a little harder. He was confident the dun was up to the challenge. He would have to be careful, though, because if the two men ahead of him were watching their back trail, they might spot him. He would have to scout out every rise before he allowed himself to be skylighted.

Longarm slid down the dune and mounted up. "All right, old son," he said to the horse. "Here's where we find out how much sand we got, and I ain't talking about this damned desert."

About fifteen minutes later, as Longarm was pushing along after the two riders, the dun suddenly jerked its head up and let out a soft whicker. Longarm had seen horses react like that before, especially in such hot, dry surroundings. Somehow, although they were in the middle of a desert, the dun had smelled water. Longarm was sure of it.

So there *was* at least one water hole out here in the *Llano Caliente*. Longarm felt a surge of excitement. The presence of water meant it might be possible after all that the stolen herds had been driven across the desert. He wasn't sure why no one in the area seemed to know about the water hole, but he could worry about that later. Right now he was facing a more urgent decision. If he let the dun have its head, there was a good chance the horse would go straight for the water. But there were those two riders up there to follow, as well. If those paths diverged . . .

Maybe they wouldn't, Longarm told himself. He had a feeling the riders belonged to the gang that had stopped those trains, and if that was the case, they almost certainly knew about the water hole. They had probably either stopped at it already or were on their way to it now. Longarm made up his mind. He would keep playing out the hand for a while longer and see what happened.

"All right, hoss," he said to the dun as he slackened his grip on the reins. "Let's find that water hole."

The dun set off at a fast walk, and with every step it seemed to become more eager to proceed. That meant the smell of the water was getting stronger. Longarm let the horse choose its own pace, and before long they were trotting over the sand dunes. He kept an eye on the tracks he had been following, and the dun's course went right along with them, confirming Longarm's guess that the two riders had been at the water hole before he spotted them. He knew now the water had to be close, or the dun wouldn't have reacted so strongly.

He topped a rise, spotted the riders about five hundred yards ahead of him, and saw them drop out of sight suddenly, as if they had spurred their horses. Longarm bit back a curse. It was possible they had been looking back and had seen him. He should have held the dun in a little, he told himself. Well, the damage, if there was any, was already done now. He let his mount continue toward the water hole.

A few minutes later, Longarm caught a whiff of water himself. It was an indefinable scent but unmistakable, even more so out here in this arid wilderness. Longarm brought the dun to a stop. The horse didn't want to be reined in, but Longarm realized he couldn't count on the water hole being deserted. If those two riders had been there recently, as seemed very likely, there was no reason others of the rustler gang couldn't still be there now. He wanted to proceed on foot. Finding one of the occasional mesquite bushes, he tied the dun's reins to a gnarled branch. The horse gave a whicker of protest. Longarm said, "Sorry, old son. Don't worry. I'll come back and get you if the coast is clear."

On foot now, the soft sand pulling at his boots as he walked, Longarm worked his way forward. He came to a particularly steep dune and had to use his hands to balance himself as he climbed it. His mouth quirked in a grimace as he touched the painfully hot sand. His toes were baking inside his boots. His mouth was so dry he could spit cotton. He hated deserts, that was for damned sure.

But this one had an oasis of sorts in the middle of it.

Longarm bellied down on the sand and took his hat off just before he reached the top of the dune. He used his toes and elbows to push himself up higher so that he could peer over the crest. On the far side, the dune swept down into one of those depressions that was clogged with mesquite bushes. This low place was even lower than usual, however, because it had a large, well-like hole in its center that was ten feet wide and deep enough so that its walls were carved out of the rock that lay underneath the sand. Carved out was the wrong way to describe it, though, Longarm thought as he stared at the well. From the looks of it, the hole had been blasted out with explosives, probably dynamite. Then the sand had been shoveled back around it and a wall made of split logs had been erected to keep the sand from funneling back in. Sunlight reflected on something at the bottom of the hole. Longarm recognized the glint of light on water. This was a well, all right, a man-made well in the middle of the desert.

"Son of a bitch," Longarm breathed. It made sense now. That shallow pool of water at the bottom of the well wouldn't be enough to satisfy a whole herd of thirsty cows, but if there were several of the wells scattered across the desert, it was possible that the stolen herds could have been driven all the way through to the Solomons on the western edge of the *Llano Caliente*. That was where he would find the stolen stock. Longarm was sure of it.

Of course, there was still the question of what the wideloopers were doing with the rustled beeves. According to Sheriff Willard, they weren't selling the cows at the stockyard in Rossville, and the Solomon Mountains, though not overly tall, were rugged enough so that driving cattle over them was out of the question.

But driving them through the desert should have been out of the question, too, and the rustlers had found a way to do that.

Longarm didn't have to follow those two riders now. He had the answer to one of his questions and had taken the first step in tracking down the gang of cattle thieves. He could return to Castleton, replenish his water, and tomorrow would head straight across the desert toward the mountains. There was a little town over there—Bell City, Longarm recalled—and that would be the next stop on his quest.

First, though, there was no reason he shouldn't fill his canteens here at the blasted-out well and let the dun have a drink as well. No one seemed to be around. He thought it would be safe enough to pay a visit to the oasis.

He went back to the dun, untied the horse, and led it over the steep dune, both of them struggling with the slope. Finally, though, they made it over, and the dun broke into a trot. To the horse's sensitive nose, the smell of the water had to be maddening by now. Longarm let him go and slid down the dune after him.

Wooden troughs had been set up around the well, so that the cattle could drink from them. The water would have be hauled up in buckets and dumped in the troughs. A few inches remained in the bottom of one of them, and the dun plunged its muzzle into the welcome moisture. Longarm let the horse drink for a minute, then grasped the halter firmly and pulled its head away from the water. "Not too much, now," he said. "Don't want you to go to foundering."

He waited, ignoring his own thirst, and after a while let the horse drink some more. Then he lashed the reins around one of the remaining mesquites in the bottom of the depression. The dun snorted. Longarm patted its flank and said, "It's for your own good, old son."

He took the empty canteens off the saddle and went to the well. A bucket hung from a rope attached to the wall. The bucket was already in the water. Longarm set the canteens on the wall beside him and reached down to grasp the rope so that he could pull up the bucket.

That was when a bullet buzzed past his ear, struck one of the empty canteens, and sent it spinning off the wall.

Chapter 6

Longarm let his instincts do the reacting for him. He flung himself to the left in a rolling dive. He heard the crack of a rifle as another slug chewed splinters from the top of the split log wall. Even as he was rolling over on the sand, his hand found the butt of his Colt and palmed the revolver out of the cross-draw rig on his left hip.

But there was nothing to shoot at. As he came up in a crouch next to the wall, his head swiveled around in search of the bushwhacker who was shooting at him. He saw nothing but sand, no matter where he looked. The buzzard could be up there on the far side of any of those dunes.

With a vicious whine, another bullet whipped past his ear. Longarm couldn't be sure, but he thought this shot came from a different direction. He saw a puff of white smoke from the crest of a dune to his left and snapped a shot toward it. Then a fourth slug smacked into the wall just to his right. The sons of bitches had him in a cross fire.

He went to his belly and crawled along the base of the wall, trying to find a spot where neither of the riflemen could reach him. He was sure there were at least two men gunning for him, and he was almost equally convinced that they were the two riders he had been following. They *had* seen him, just as he'd feared, and they had doubled back to the well in a hurry, no doubt thinking they would find their pursuer there. And they'd been right, much to Longarm's chagrin.

The problem was, it was so damned hard to think straight in this heat. He had let his thirst, and that of his horse, get the better of him, and it looked like he might pay for that momentary lapse with his life.

The rifles cracked from opposite sides of the depression where the well was located. As Longarm hunkered even lower to the ground, he cast a glance toward the dun, which was dancing around skittishly, probably getting ready to bolt. His Winchester was there, snugged into a sheath attached to the saddle. With it in his hands, he might be able to make a fight of it, despite having the odds against him. Armed only with a six-gun, he stood little if any chance against the pair of bushwhackers. They could shift around all they wanted up there, safe behind the walls of sand, until sooner or later one of them would have a clear shot at him. There was no place to hide.

Except, he realized, in the well itself.

Even as that thought went through his head, another bullet crashed into the wall less than a foot away from him.

Biting back a curse, Longarm jammed his Colt in its holster and pushed himself upward. A slug plucked at his shirtsleeve as he slapped both hands on the wall and vaulted over it. His hat came off his head as he fell into the well, dropping the eight feet or so to the water. He landed with a huge splash.

The water in the bottom of the well was several feet deep, but he still hit hard against the stone floor beneath the water. The stuff was sandy, and he tasted grit in his mouth and felt it in his nose as his head went under. He came up shaking his head and pawing at his eyes to clear them. With a sinking sensation, he realized he had only postponed his doom. All the two riflemen had to do now was skulk up to the edge of the well and poke their weapons over the wall. Then they could blast him to their hearts' content.

Longarm looked at the curving walls around him. The surfaces were irregular, the results of the explosions that had blasted this well out of the desert rock. Under different circumstances, it wouldn't have been much trouble to find enough handholds and footholds so that he could climb out of here. As it was, though, climbing out would mean climbing right back into the gunsights of the two hombres who wanted him dead. He might be able to hold them off for a little while as they approached the well, but it wouldn't be long before he was out of bullets. He had the four rounds still in the cylinder of his Colt, plus another dozen cartridges in the loops of his gunbelt. Luckily, being dunked in the well wouldn't have any effect on the metallic rounds, though the sandy water wouldn't be good for the workings of the revolver. He would have to worry about cleaning it later—assuming there *was* a later, and right now the chances of that were looking pretty damned slim.

A few more shots smacked into the wall around the well before the bushwhackers figured out they were wasting ammunition. The shooting died away, to be replaced with a silence broken only by the soft sighing of the desert wind.

Longarm listened intently, thinking he would be able to hear boots crunching on the sand as the gunmen approached. Instead, after a few minutes, a man's voice called out to him. "Hey! You there in the well! You hear me, cowboy?"

Without responding, Longarm waited to see what the men would do. He didn't have to wait for long. With a note of impatience in his voice, the man who had spoken before called again.

"Listen, you damn fool! Nobody has to die here! Just climb out of that well and put your hands up! Better toss out your six-shooter first, though!"

If he did that, they would ventilate him as soon as they had a clear shot at him, Longarm knew. He was convinced they were part of the gang of rustlers, and now that he knew of the well's existence, they couldn't afford to let him live. He could ruin the whole scheme for them by going back to Castleton and explaining how the stolen herds had made it across the barren *Llano Caliente*. The two would-be killers probably had no idea that he was a lawman, but that wouldn't matter. He would have been a threat to their operation even if he had been just a wandering cowpoke.

Longarm's heart thudded heavily in his chest. All he could do was wait here at the bottom of the well and try to lure them out so that he could get a shot at them. If they were foolish enough to stick their heads over the wall, he planned to put bullets right between their eyes.

Of course, that wasn't going to happen. They wouldn't have to look into the well in order to shoot into it. They could just slip up to the wall and pour lead down into the water until nothing could be alive down here.

Still he said nothing, not wanting to give them the satisfaction of knowing they had him trapped. They might try to make him beg for his life, and that wasn't going to happen. Not in a month of Sundays. He waited and listened, and a few minutes later he was rewarded by the sound of voices, closer now to the well. Sounds carried well in the dry desert air, and he could make out most of what they were saying.

". . . got to take care of him . . . let him live, Culhane'll have our hides."

"Culhane ain't the one . . . stick his head over that . . . get it blowed off."

Culhane. Longarm made a mental note of the name, even though it seemed unlikely he would ever have the chance to make use of it. The way the two men were talking, this gent Culhane was their boss, the leader of the rustlers.

". . . got to do is . . . can't hit us from down in there . . . shoot until . . . got to be dead."

Longarm grimaced. They had it figured out, all right. And as soon as they worked up the nerve to crawl up to the well, his remaining time would be numbered in minutes, if not seconds.

The long, silent moments drew out, stretching Longarm's nerves with them. A part of him wanted to clamber up that wall, throw himself over, and blaze away at the gunmen, even though he knew he would be riddled with bullets if he tried that. He was going to be shot to pieces soon enough anyway. Might as well try to take one of the bastards with him. He figured he had a chance to do that before he went down.

His muscles were tensed, ready to move, when he heard the sudden sharp whipcrack of another rifle, farther away than the voices of the gunmen had been. One of them cried out in pain, and the other one yelled, "What the hell?"

The third rifle continued to bark, and Longarm almost would have sworn that he recognized the sound of its reports. It sounded just like the Winchester he carried. In a voice choked by pain, the killer who had cried out called, "Help me, Roy! Give me a han—*Uhhh!*"

The ugly thud of a bullet striking flesh had come just a split-instant before that grunt of mortal agony. Longarm figured the wounded man had been hit again, even worse this time. And judging from the rapid patter of boots slapping against the sand, the other gunman, under fire now, was beating a hasty retreat and leaving his wounded companion behind.

Longarm reached up, found a couple of handholds, and started pulling himself toward the top of the well. He heard a scattering of pistol shots, a few more cracks from the rifle, and then nothing. Silence fell over the depression again. Longarm kept climbing.

He paused just below the top, hung on with one hand and the toes of his boots while he unlimbered the Colt with the other hand. Then, with the muscles in his shoulders and back bunching from the effort, he hauled himself up and over the wall, tumbling onto the ground next to the well. He threw himself into a roll in case anybody was trying to draw a bead on him and ended up a few feet away, lying on his belly with his head up and the revolver poised in his hand.

He wouldn't be needing the gun to deal with the man who lay on the sand a few feet away from him. That poor son of a bitch was already dead.

The man stared sightlessly at Longarm. He was sprawled on his back, his neck twisted. A red-rimmed black hole was punched in his forehead just above his left eye. Longarm couldn't see the back of the man's head, but he figured where the bullet had come out wasn't nearly as neat as where it had gone in. The man's shirt was bloody on the right side where he had been hit first. Longarm didn't know and didn't care if that wound would have proven fatal; the bullet through the bastard's brain had removed any doubt.

The man was dressed in range clothes that had seen better days. The garb was fairly clean, though, and the man had shaved recently. His features, contorted now in death, had been hard in life, Longarm judged. He didn't look exactly like the typical drifting outlaw, though. Tough and salty, sure, but more like a top cowhand than somebody riding the owlhoot trail. This hombre had a home.

That was unusual, but nothing Longarm cared to ponder right now. He looked around for the other bushwhacker, but the fella was gone. He had taken off for the tall and uncut—not that there was any such thing out here in the desert—as soon as he realized he was in danger of being gunned down like his partner had been.

Longarm's lineback dun was gone, too. The horse had finally taken off, spooked by the shooting. Longarm was glad the critter had had that much sense. Sure, he was afoot right now, but he hoped he could follow the dun's tracks and catch up to it. There was the little matter of whoever had saved him from nearly certain death, too. Longarm was mighty curious who the Good Samaritan was.

He found out a few moments later, and the revelation came as quite a shock. A rider appeared at the top of one of the dunes and rode down toward the well, leading the dun. The denim-clad figure was slender and wore a broad-brimmed straw hat. On the way down, the hat slipped back and hung on its neck strap, and Longarm stared as he recognized Elizabeth Townsend.

"Good Lord, gal," Longarm exclaimed as she rode up to the well. "What are you doing here?"

She was staring at the dead man as she reined in, and her eyes were wide with horror. Longarm moved so that he was between her and the corpse. That seemed to break the spell. Elizabeth said, "Custis? Are you all right?"

Longarm looked down at himself. He was soaked from being in the well, but the wet clothes didn't feel too bad in this heat. In fact, they were sort of refreshing. And he wasn't dead, which was saying quite a bit. He grinned at Elizabeth and said, "I'm a whole heap better than I expected to be right about now, thanks to you. I reckon you're the one who opened fire on those gents who were trying to kill me?"

She nodded, being careful now not to look at the dead man. "I heard the shots and then found the dun running loose, and I knew you had to be in trouble. So I got your rifle and rode up on top of that dune. When I saw those men creeping up on this . . . this well, I figured you must be inside there." She looked in amazement at the well. "I never saw such a thing."

"Folks have been digging wells for thousands of years," Longarm said. "The fellas who dug this one used dynamite to do it, I reckon. I figure there are a few more just like it between here and the mountains over to the west."

Elizabeth looked hard at him. "You don't work for a land and cattle syndicate, do you, Custis?"

Longarm hesitated, then shook his head. "Nope. And I hope you don't take it too unkindly that I stretched the truth with you. I'm a deputy U.S. marshal, on the trail of those cow thieves who've been stopping the trains hereabouts."

"I've heard all about that," Elizabeth said. "Sheriff Willard comes to the house sometimes to visit with Dad and play dominoes with him and Alf. The story is that those stolen herds were driven into the desert and then disappeared."

"They didn't disappear," Longarm said, his voice grim. "The rustlers watered them at these tanks and drove them on across. I ain't figured out the rest of it yet, but that's the start of it." He rubbed his jaw. "You still ain't told me how come you happened to be riding around in the *Llano Caliente* just when I needed you to give me a hand."

"I got worried about you. I managed to worm it out of Uncle Stan—I mean Sheriff Willard; he's not really my uncle—that you had come out here into the desert with enough water to last you all day. I was worried you might get lost, though. I know the *Llano Caliente* about as well as anybody around here, so I thought I would make sure you were all right." She looked at the well again and shook her head. "I sure didn't know about this, though. It can't have been here for very long."

"Six months or so," Longarm said. "That's how long the rustling's been going on."

Elizabeth nodded, clearly agreeing with his logic.

"I don't reckon I can thank you enough for what you did," Longarm went on. "You saved my life."

"I'm just glad I came along in time to help."

Longarm took the reins of the dun from her. As he moved forward, the body of the dead man was revealed again. Though he hated to do it, he had to ask her, "Have you ever seen that fella before?"

Elizabeth took a deep breath and gave the corpse a good long look. Then she turned her gaze to Longarm as he swung up into the saddle on the dun's back. "He looks familiar somehow," she said. "Like I've seen him a time or two but don't really know him. Does he look like an outlaw to you?"

"I ain't sure," Longarm replied. "He was sure enough ready to kill me in cold blood, him and his pard both. He may not look the part, but he's an owlhoot, no doubt about that. You know anybody named Culhane?"

"Culhane?" Elizabeth repeated. "I'm not sure. It's like that . . . that dead man. There's something familiar about it, but I can't put my finger on it. Who's this Culhane supposed to be?"

"The way those two bushwhackers were talking while they were skulking up to the well, Culhane's their boss. Don't worry, I'll find him. Right now, we'd best get back to Castleton."

Elizabeth looked up at the sky, where the sun was low in the west and orange and gold streaks were painted across the heavens. "I'm not sure we can get back to town before dark."

"Well, I want to get away from here, anyway," Long-arm said.

Elizabeth cast one more glance at the corpse and gave a tiny shudder. "So do I," she said.

Chapter 7

Nightfall found them still on the desert, as Elizabeth had suggested it would. As the stars came out, appearing as pinpricks of light against the sable sky, Longarm reined in and called a halt.

"We'll be able to see well enough to ride in a little while," Elizabeth said. "Once the moon's up, there'll be plenty of light."

"That won't be for a spell yet," Longarm said, "and in the meantime, these horses could use some rest, especially the dun. I'm a mite weary myself."

Elizabeth slid down from her saddle. "I'm not surprised. Gallivanting all over the desert and getting yourself shot at like that. It's hard work."

Longarm grinned at her teasing, unoffended by it. He was glad to see that she seemed to have recovered a bit from the shock of killing a man.

He dismounted and took down one of the canteens from the saddle. Before leaving the well, they had refilled all the canteens they had, the ones he'd brought with him as well as the pair tied onto Elizabeth's saddle. Longarm unscrewed the cap and took a swig, making a face at the sand that was swirling around in the water. Even though it was a little gritty, it was still wet, and that was all that mattered.

Elizabeth took off her hat and poured water from one of the canteens into it so that the horses could drink. She was riding a chestnut gelding that seemed to be a good horse, though Longarm doubted that it had as much staying power as the dun.

Longarm's hat was still somewhere in the bottom of that well. He hadn't wanted to climb back in there and feel around for it under the water. When they got back to Castleton, he would buy himself a new one. Henry might complain about it when Longarm added the cost of a new hat onto his expenses for this mission, but that was just too bad. Since he'd lost it while those bushwhackers were trying to kill him, he figured it was in the line of duty.

They had stopped near some of the mesquite bushes. The horses wandered over to nibble on the beans. Elizabeth stretched to relieve weary muscles, then sat down on the sand. "We ought to be back in Castleton by midnight," she said.

Longarm sank to the ground beside her. The sand was still plenty warm underneath him, but it was a lot cooler than it had been during the day. Once the sun was down, the heat stored up in the sand was dissipated in a hurry by the dry air and the night breezes. The sand would remain pleasantly warm for a while, but by morning it would be cold, like the rest of the desert. Longarm supposed that at that time of day, *Llano Frio* would be a more appropriate name for this place.

Elizabeth leaned against him, resting her head on his shoulder. "I'm so glad I found you when I did, Custis," she murmured.

"When those sidewinders had me trapped in that well, you mean?"

"Yes, I suppose so. But I'm glad you came to Castleton when you did, too. Now that I've met you . . . well, I guess you've helped tame the restlessness in me. I don't feel so desperate to get out and do something different. I suppose all of your experiences have rubbed off on me a little."

Longarm frowned in the darkness. "I ain't so sure that's a good thing," he said. "Everybody needs to be a little fiddle-footed in their soul. Life has more spice that way, even if you never get the chance to traipse all over to hell and gone."

"But if you never get the chance to do those things, wouldn't that make you awfully frustrated?"

"I reckon it could," Longarm said. "I wouldn't know from experience, because I've always moved around a lot and stayed busy in my work. But it just seems to me that it's better for folks to dream, even if those dreams never come true."

After a moment, Elizabeth said, "Because the dead don't dream."

"That's one way of looking at it," Longarm said.

She sighed. He put his arm around her shoulders and drew her closer. After a few minutes, it seemed inevitable that she would lift her face to his and he would kiss her. That was exactly what happened. While he was kissing her, Longarm put his other arm around her, lifting and turning her so that she was straddling his lap. His fingers went to the buttons of her shirt and began to unfasten them. When he had them undone, he spread the shirt open and cupped her small, firm left breast in his right hand. Elizabeth reached down between them and found the bulge at his groin. While Longarm gently massaged the warm flesh of her breast, she worked at the buttons of his trousers and freed his shaft. It jutted up between them, long and thick and proud, and she filled her hands with it, sliding them up and down along the pole.

Elizabeth broke the kiss and whispered, "I need you in me again, Custis."

"I reckon we've got time for that," Longarm said. "The moon won't be up for a while yet."

Elizabeth's fingers tightened on his manhood. "And since *you're* already up . . ."

Longarm laughed. Elizabeth was quite a gal. She stood up and unbuckled her belt, then unbuttoned her denim trousers and slid them down over her hips and thighs. She kicked her legs free of them. Squatting and straddling Longarm's lap again, she grasped his shaft and aimed the head of it straight at the core of her femaleness. Taking her time, she sank down on it, letting the thick pole of flesh fill her. At last he was sheathed completely within her. She gave her hips a little bounce and gasped at the sensations the movement created inside her. "Oh, my goodness," she said. "This is wonderful."

Longarm couldn't argue with that. Elizabeth's shirt was still hanging open. He bent his head to her right breast and drew the erect nipple into his mouth. His tongue circled the hard little bud surrounded by a ring of brown, pebbled flesh. Opening his mouth wider, he sucked in even more of the soft breast. Elizabeth stroked his head, running her fingers through his dark brown hair. After a while, Longarm moved his lips and tongue to her other nipple. She gave a contented sigh.

They sat still for the most part, each of them savoring the feeling of having his manhood buried so deeply inside her. At last, though, the urgings of their passion became too great to withstand. Elizabeth began to move her hips back and forth, and Longarm responded by thrusting in and out of her with deliberate, almost lazy strokes. He slid his arms around her waist and tightened his embrace.

As the minutes passed, the pace of their lovemaking gradually grew faster. Longarm's heart pounded in his chest. Elizabeth gasped again and threw her head back. He raised his head from her breasts and kissed the hollow of her throat, the line of her jaw, the point of her chin, and finally her mouth. All the while, he continued pumping his shaft in and out of her, and she met each of his thrusts with one of her own. They climbed higher and higher together, ascending toward the peak that each wanted so much to share with the other.

Feeling his climax about to wash over him, Longarm drove as deeply into her as he could and then held himself there, so that when his seed erupted from him, it flooded the innermost depths of her core. He felt the gushing flow of her own culmination drenching him. She cried out and clutched at his shoulders as she rode him. Her lips found his and her tongue darted into his mouth. For long, dizzying moments, they were as close to being merged into one being as two people could get.

Elizabeth went limp, sagging into his arms with a low moan of utter satisfaction. Longarm tightened his arms around her and lay back on the sand, cradling her slender form atop his body. His shaft was still buried inside her. It spasmed one final time, causing her to say, "Oh," in a hollow voice. After that, neither of them had the strength to talk for a while.

At last, as Longarm looked over Elizabeth's shoulder, he saw a rounded golden orb peeking over one of the sand dunes. "Moon's up," he said.

"Let it get higher," she said. "I don't think I can move right now."

Longarm nodded. Waiting a while was all right with him, too.

But as he lay there stroking her flanks and relishing the way she started kissing his chest as she lay on top of him, he felt himself growing hard again. Elizabeth felt it, too, of course, and she raised her head to say, "Custis . . . ?"

Longarm put a hand on each side of her face and kissed her. "I reckon you're what they call an inspiration."

"Oh, my God. You're definitely getting . . . inspired."

So he was, and over the next few minutes, they dis-

76

covered that Elizabeth had been wrong about something. She was still able to move after all. In fact, thought Longarm, she moved just fine . . .

Later, they rode on through the night toward the edge of the *Llano Caliente*. Longarm felt good about the way things had worked out. Given the fact that he had been plucked out of a death trap earlier in the day, he had to be optimistic about the way his luck was running. And he was confident that once he got to Bell City and explored the narrow strip of cattle range over there between the desert and the mountains, he would find out what had happened to the missing herds.

"You won't be staying in Castleton for very long once we get back, will you?" Elizabeth asked. The question made Longarm realize that she had been thinking about some of the same things he had been mulling over.

"No, I'll have to get on about my business," he replied honestly. "But when I've got this case wrapped up, I'll do my best to hang around for a couple of days, if my boss don't order me back to Denver right away because he's got another job waiting for me."

"You'll try to stay for a couple of days . . . so you can say a proper good-bye to me, is that it?"

Longarm frowned, then said, "I won't lie to you, Elizabeth. I think a whole heap too much of you to do that. I ain't the type to settle down in one place for too long. I've been moving around most of my life, and I don't reckon I can stop now."

She laughed, but it had a slightly hollow sound to it. "Well, you're an honest man, at least."

"I try to be," Longarm said.

"And even though saying good-bye to you will be hard, I'd rather have had you around for a few days than not at all, Custis. That's how much being with you has meant to me."

77

"I'm mighty glad to hear that."

Elizabeth sighed. "My God, I'll bet you've broken some hearts over the years, Custis Long."

"Never on purpose, though."

"No," she agreed, "you wouldn't do that."

They rode on in silence for a few minutes. Longarm thought they ought to be getting close to the edge of the desert. He was about to say as much when he heard an unexpected sound floating on the night air. It was the whinny of a horse.

Without thinking too much about what he was doing, he leaned forward and reached around the dun's head to grab its nose and silence any reply. He was about to hiss at Elizabeth to do the same thing, but it was too late. Her chestnut lifted its head and pealed out a long, shrill whinny in response to the other horse that was out there somewhere in the night. "Damn it!" Longarm grated as he reined the dun to an abrupt halt.

"Custis!" Elizabeth exclaimed. "What's wrong?" She followed his lead and brought the chestnut to a stop.

"There's another horse up ahead, and it caught our animals' scents. Where there's a horse, there's usually a rider."

"So?"

"It ain't likely we'll run into any friends out here. The last two fellas I crossed paths with tried to kill me."

Elizabeth's face was tense in the moonlight. "You can't be sure whoever is up there is one of the outlaws. Maybe it's Sheriff Willard. He might have gotten worried and come to look for me."

Quickly, Longarm considered the suggestion. He realized that he couldn't rule it out. Even if Elizabeth hadn't told Willard she was coming into the desert to look for him, the lawman was smart enough to figure that out from the questions she had asked him.

They couldn't call out, though, because if the other

night rider wasn't Willard, that would be giving away their position. Of course, Elizabeth's horse had pretty much done that already. Longarm's jaw tightened. The good luck he had been thinking about earlier seemed to be slipping away in a hurry now. That was usually the way things went.

He pulled the Winchester from the saddle boot and sat there for a long moment, listening intently. He hadn't heard the other horse make a sound since that first whinny. That didn't bode well. That meant the horse's rider was keeping it quiet for some reason, and it couldn't be anything good.

"Get down," Longarm said to Elizabeth in a half-whisper.

He swung down from the saddle and she did likewise. Longarm handed the dun's reins to her. "You lead the horses," he told her. "If there's any shooting, drop the dun's reins, jump up on that chestnut, and get the hell out of here. Head east and sift sand as hard as you can."

"But Custis, I couldn't just leave—"

"Blast it, do what I tell you!" he said. "Now come on."

He started forward on foot, moving as silently and carefully as an Indian. Elizabeth followed behind, making more noise with the horses, but that couldn't be helped. Longarm's hands were tight on the rifle, ready to put it to instant use.

In addition to listening, he also sniffed the air as he went forward, alert for the scent of tobacco smoke. The fact that he didn't smell anything wasn't necessarily a good sign. Anybody who was out here in the desert on an innocent errand would be liable to roll and light up a quirly. But a smart man who was stalking another man wouldn't light up or allow anyone with him to do so, for fear that the smell of smoke would give away their presence.

Or maybe he was just being too damned suspicious,

Longarm told himself. Not everything had to be a clue or have some deeper meaning. Sometimes, no smoke was just no smoke.

It was right about then that riders boiled over sand dunes to the right and left, galloping and shooting.

Chapter 8

Longarm shouted, "Elizabeth! Get out of here!" as he flung the rifle to his shoulder. He worked the lever as he brought the weapon up, jacking a cartridge into the chamber. Centering the sights on one of the onrushing horsemen to the right as best he could in the moonlight, he pulled the trigger.

The crack of the rifle echoed over the sand. By the time the echo began to die away, Longarm had shifted his aim and fired three more times, creating a sound like the roll of thunder. Added to the bark of the rifle was the popping of handguns from the riders. Powdersmoke hazed the air. Longarm couldn't tell if any of his shots had found their targets or not, but there were still plenty of gunmen charging toward him.

These men were members of Culhane's gang. He was sure of it. The one who had gotten away back at the well had made it to their hideout and told Culhane that a stranger had discovered the secret of the *Llano Caliente*. Knowing that they couldn't afford to let Longarm reach Castleton, Culhane and his men had fogged it back across the desert and set up this ambush. That chain of logic formed in an instant in Longarm's brain as bullets flew around him, and he knew it made sense.

He threw a glance over his shoulder to make sure Elizabeth had fled. To his dismay, he saw that while she had leaped on the chestnut as he had instructed her to, the horse was dancing around in a panic and Elizabeth was having a hard time bringing it under control. The animal was so spooked by the fusillade of gunfire that even a very experienced rider like Elizabeth couldn't calm it down.

The dun was skittish, too. Longarm hated to use such a fine mount as a living shield, but he ducked behind the dun, grabbed its reins, and thrust the barrel of the Winchester across the saddle, putting the horse between him and the bushwhackers. He fired twice more, and this time he saw one of the killers go flying out of the saddle. He thought he saw a couple of other riderless horses, too, but it was hard to be sure with all the dust and powdersmoke in the air, obscuring the moonlight.

The chestnut screamed, and Longarm jerked his head around to see the horse toppling onto its side, obviously hit. "Elizabeth!" he shouted. If the horse fell on her, she would be crushed.

She kept her head, though, and kicked her feet free of the stirrups. Longarm felt a surge of relief as he saw her go sailing out of the saddle to land in a rolling sprawl on the sand.

That relief was very short-lived. They were still in a mess of trouble. He snapped a couple more shots at the attackers, who were pulling back now, their first charge blunted by Longarm's deadly accuracy with the Winchester. Darting to Elizabeth's side, he bent, got an arm around her waist, and hauled her to her feet.

"You've gotta get out of here!" he said.

"No, Custis!"

He lifted her bodily, practically threw her onto the back

of the dun. She grabbed at the horse's mane to keep herself in the saddle. Longarm didn't waste any time. He slapped the dun's rump and yelled, *"Hyaaaah!"*

The mouse-colored horse with the darker stripe down its back leaped forward. Elizabeth swayed back and forth, jolted by the horse's sudden start, but she managed to stay on the dun's back. She headed for the top of the dune behind them. Longarm was between her and the outlaws, and that was the way he wanted it.

He scrambled over to the fallen chestnut. The gelding was dead, cut down by outlaw bullets. Longarm threw himself behind the horse, stretching out prone on the sand and thrusting the barrel of the Winchester over the sleek-hided flank of the dead animal.

His heart thudded wildly in his chest. He took a couple of deep breaths to calm himself. He was in a mighty bad fix for the second time today. If the outlaws charged him head-on again, he could pick off some of them from behind the shelter of the dead horse and make them pay for overrunning him. But in the end, overrunning him was exactly what they would do. He couldn't hold off the whole bunch of them.

On the other hand, if Culhane didn't want to pay that high a price, he could send men circling around to either or both sides, so that they would have clear shots at Longarm from above and behind him. And there wasn't a damned thing he could do to stop that. At least the outlaws were hesitating a few minutes, trying to figure out what to do, and that would give Elizabeth a chance to escape. Longarm could still hear the hoofbeats of the dun. He turned his head and gazed behind him, seeing Elizabeth and the horse as a single dark shape in the silvery moonlight, moving against the light-colored sand as they neared the top of the dune they were climbing.

A shot rang out from somewhere nearby, and Longarm shouted, "No!" as he saw Elizabeth fall from the saddle, her arms outflung. She toppled off the dun and fell in a limp sprawl, rolling several yards back down the slope before coming to a stop.

Longarm's pulse hammered crazily inside his skull. His eyes were wide with horror. He couldn't believe what he had just seen. Elizabeth had been within just a few yards of escaping when she was cut down so cruelly. Earlier today, she had saved his life. . . .

And now he had cost her hers.

The world turned blood red in front of Longarm's eyes. It was as if the silver glow of the moon floating high overhead had been replaced by the garish gleam of hell's own eternal fire and brimstone. With an incoherent shout of rage, he came up on his knees and blazed away at the dunes around him, firing as fast as he could work the Winchester's lever. At the same time he bellowed curses at the outlaws, though he was barely aware of that. Only the click of the rifle's hammer on an empty chamber brought him back to his senses, and as he realized what he was doing, he heard bullets zinging around him and saw muzzle flashes from the dunes.

"Hold your fire!" someone shouted behind him. "Stop shooting, damn it!"

Longarm twisted around and saw three men charging toward him. They had crept around the dunes, just as he expected they would, and now they were attacking from the other direction. He dropped the empty rifle and grabbed for his Colt.

"I want him alive!" the same man shouted.

It was a mighty nice time to decide that, Longarm thought fleetingly, after the gang had thrown several hundred rounds at him. He brought up his revolver and snapped off a shot. Flame lanced into the darkness as one of the outlaws returned fire. What felt like a giant fist clubbed Longarm in the side and knocked him halfway around. He fired the Colt again and saw one of the onrushing outlaws driven backward by the slug. Then the other two were on him. A booted foot swung in a vicious kick that caught him on the wrist and sent the revolver spinning away out of his hand. The other man slashed at his head with a gun barrel. Longarm ducked under the blow and threw himself forward in a diving tackle, catching the man around the knees. Both of them went down.

Longarm was losing strength in a hurry, and he knew it. His right side had gone numb when he was first hit by a bullet, but now spears of agony began to shoot through him as he wrestled with the man he had knocked down. He heard frantic footsteps scuffling around him and knew his remaining time was numbered in seconds. He threw a punch with his left hand, felt it crunch into a face with a satisfying impact.

Then the world landed on the back of his head. The moonlight was gone, and so was the red, nightmarish hellfire that had replaced it. Nothing was left except blackness, and Longarm tumbled forward into it, falling for an eternity.

"He killed Nate and Otis. I say we plug him and be done with it."

"Then it's a good thing you don't make the decisions around here, Lewis. I want to find out who this hombre is and who he might have told about those wells."

"I don't think he had a chance to tell anybody, boss, except maybe that other gent who was with him. And he's dead."

"Maybe. But I've got to be sure. I can't have anything going wrong. Not now. Not after we've worked so hard and waited so long."

The words were clear enough to understand, but the voices seemed to come from far, far away. Longarm listened to them but really didn't think about what they were saying. Nor did he consider the implications of the fact that he was hearing several men speaking. It was quite a while after that before he realized that the voices meant he was still alive.

He was being bounced and jolted around, and with each bounce and jolt came a fresh stab of pain. After several minutes—or hours, or days, he wasn't sure which—he figured out that he was on a horse, tied face down over the saddle. His side where the bullet had hit him was a mass of agony. He was sick, too, his stomach roiling around and threatening to empty itself. With an effort, he quelled that notion. If he vomited, the men riding around him might figure out that he was conscious, and he didn't want that yet.

He forced his thoughts to work in something like a normal manner, cutting through the fog of pain that gripped his brain. Thinking back on the exchange he had overheard just as he was regaining consciousness, he assigned the second voice to the man called Culhane, the leader of this gang of rustlers and killers. Culhane had come after him intending to kill him, but at the last minute the boss outlaw had changed his mind. Culhane wanted to make sure Longarm hadn't passed on the secret of the *Llano Caliente* to anyone else, as unlikely as that possibility seemed.

A fresh wave of pain hit him, but this one wasn't physical. It was deep in his soul, and it was a mixture of grief and anger over the death of Elizabeth Townsend. If she hadn't come into the desert after him . . . if he hadn't ever gotten involved with her in the first place . . . she would still be alive, running the livery stable in Castleton and taking care of her invalid father. Dreaming dreams that might never come true. But alive.

Longarm's teeth ground together as he fought to swallow the livid curses that tried to well up his throat. He wanted to lambaste the callous killers around him, but again, to do so would be to tip them off that he was awake. Even though his thinking was still pretty fuzzy, far in the back of his mind a clear, calm voice was urging him to stay in control of himself. That part of his brain stubbornly refused to give up, despite the fact that he was wounded and in the hands of his enemies.

Something nibbled around the edges of his consciousness, a feeling that something else was wrong, that he had missed something he should have seen or heard and understood what it meant. But after several minutes of trying to figure out what it was, he gave up. He was too weak from loss of blood, too stunned by everything that had happened, to do anything other than go where the outlaws were taking him.

That would be their hideout, he thought. He was going to find out what had happened to those stolen cows. Of course, he wouldn't be able to do anything about it. As soon as Culhane was convinced that the mysterious stranger no longer represented a threat, Longarm would be killed. A quick bullet through the head if he was lucky; maybe some red-hot knives if he wasn't.

No, they wouldn't torture him, he told himself. They weren't Apaches or Utes or Blackfeet. The Indians had refined the infliction of suffering to an art. These outlaws would just blow his brains out and be done with it.

Longarm became aware that the air around him was very cold, so cold that he began to shiver a little. He couldn't stop the reaction, but he didn't think his captors would notice it. The frigidness that gripped him could mean one of two things: Either he had lost so much blood that he was on the verge of dying from it, or it was close to dawn, when the desert was at its coldest. Or some combination of the two. Or perhaps he was just so delirious he didn't know whether he was cold or hot. Nothing had much real meaning except the pain.

He slipped away again, losing consciousness. When he came to the second time, it was with a jerk of his body and a sharply indrawn breath. The voice that he thought of as Culhane's snapped, "Hold it! That son of a bitch is awake."

The horse carrying Longarm came to a stop as one of the outlaws jerked on its reins. Longarm's head swam dizzily and he felt sick again. This time he couldn't stop himself from retching, but it no longer mattered. His captors already knew he was awake. And since he had eaten very little all day, his stomach was pretty much empty. The dry heaves shook him, left him trembling and drenched in sweat despite the coldness of the air.

"Get him down off of there," Culhane said.

Longarm felt the tug of a knife blade against the ropes that bound his wrists and ankles together under the belly of the horse. With his limbs freed, he slid off the saddle and fell hard to the ground. The impact made him feel like somebody had taken a crosscut saw to his wounded side. He lay there huddled on the sand, trying not to curl up into a ball. He didn't want to give the bastards the satisfaction of seeing how much he was hurting.

He realized now that his hands and feet had been numbed by the tight bonds, because more pain jabbed through them as the blood started to flow again. The life-giving liquid was moving sluggishly through his veins, but at least it was still moving. His brain was pretty sluggish, too. As long seconds crept past, he remembered everything that had happened earlier, including the way Elizabeth had been shot off her horse. The anger that arose in him at that memory helped to blunt the physical agony he was experiencing. He allowed the rage to well up, and as it did, it forced the pain farther back into the recesses of his mind.

Longarm heard boots crunching on the sand and opened his eyes to see one of the outlaws walking over and kneeling beside him. He couldn't make out the features of the man's face. The outlaw was just a dark silhouette looming above him, blotting out a man-sized portion of the stars. The voice was familiar, though, as the man said, "Welcome back to life, mister. Looked for a while there like you were a goner."

Longarm made no mistake about it: he *was* a goner. At least, that was what the outlaws intended. Culhane went on, "Better answer a few questions, and then we'll get you some help."

Longarm knew better than to believe that. The only assistance these men would give him would be a push into the next world, once they had found out what they wanted to know. He wanted to tell Culhane to go to hell, but he couldn't summon up the energy to do so.

"Who are you? What are you doing out here in the desert?"

Longarm didn't say anything.

"You're not helping yourself," Culhane said, and this time his voice had a harder edge to it. "You'd better face facts, my friend. You've got a bullet hole in your side, you've lost a lot of blood, and your only chance to survive is to cooperate with us. Now I'll ask you again. Who are you?"

Longarm didn't answer, but he thought about what he was hearing. Culhane's voice was smooth, educated. He wasn't a run-of-the-mill rustler and killer, the crude, ignorant sort who was not equipped mentally or emotionally for anything except a life of crime. At one time in his life, Culhane had been better than that.

Now, of course, he was a cold-blooded murderer and thief, no matter what he had been in the past.

"What were you doing at that well?" Culhane demanded. His patience ran out, and he brought his fist around, smashing it into Longarm's jaw. The blow drove Longarm's head so far to the side that sand got into his mouth. He spat out blood and grit. Compared to everything he had gone through so far, the punch was nothing.

89

He laughed, a dry, rasping chuckle. Culhane said, "Bastard," stood up, and kicked him in the side. The wounded side.

Longarm gasped, and this time he couldn't stop himself from curling up. Culhane kicked him again, in the back. The boss outlaw jerked out a revolver, pointed it at Longarm's head, and said, "How about if I just blow your damned brains out?"

One of the other men gathered around the bloody and battered lawman said, "That's a good idea, boss."

Over the din of imps inside his skull, Longarm heard a long, indrawn breath and realized it came from Culhane. The outlaw leader was regaining control of himself after that momentary lapse into crazed anger. "No," Culhane said, "I still want to know who he is. We'll take him to the ranch and work on him there. Get him back on that horse and tie his hands to the horn."

Longarm felt hands lifting him, roughly tossing him onto the back of the mount he had been on earlier. This time, however, he was allowed to sit in the saddle instead of being thrown belly down over it. Cords were lashed around his wrists, binding them to the saddle horn. He slumped forward, unable to sit upright because of the wound in his side.

The little caravan of rustlers and their lone captive set out again across the desert. Longarm already knew that they were still in the *Llano Caliente*, but as he peered through slitted eyes ahead of him, he figured out they were going west instead of east. A slight turn of his head told him that the sky behind them was growing lighter with the approach of dawn. Except for the brief stop when Culhane questioned him, they must have been riding all night. He looked ahead again, thought he saw a low, dark line on the horizon. The Solomon Mountains? Longarm thought it likely.

Culhane had said something about taking him to a

ranch. Longarm pieced that together with everything he had found out already and thought that the picture was becoming clearer. Culhane must own a ranch over there in that strip of rangeland between the desert and the Solomons. He had masterminded the rustling of the cattle off the stock trains, brought the stolen herds across the desert by way of the dynamited wells, and now had that extra stock hidden on his ranch. If Culhane had a reputation as a respectable cattleman, he could stash the extra stock on his own range without being suspected, at least for a while. Something Sheriff Willard had said popped up in Longarm's memory. There was talk of building a spur line from the railroad junction at Rossville up to Bell City. If and when that happened, Culhane could ship out the stolen stock with no one being the wiser, especially if he was patient about it and didn't dump all of them on the market at the same time. Longarm figured Culhane was too smart to do that.

The whole picture made sense now. Longarm knew there might be minor variations in Culhane's scheme that he had gotten wrong, but he was confident that, for the most part, he had figured out the answers to the questions that had brought him to this part of the country.

Fat lot of good those answers would do him, though, while he was still Culhane's prisoner. He had to get away somehow. Wounded as he was, he couldn't hope to take on a whole gang of rustlers and killers. But if he could reach another lawman, or somehow get word to Billy Vail to send him some help, then Culhane's days as an outlaw kingpin would be over.

The only problem was going to be getting away before Culhane got tired of waiting around and killed him.

Chapter 9

As the sky grew still lighter, Longarm began to be able to make out the mountains in the distance. It was difficult to tell how far away they were, especially with his eyesight a little fuzzy from all the punishment he had endured during the past eighteen hours. He thought the rounded, rocky peaks were getting closer, though. The group of riders ought to be reaching the edge of the desert before too much longer, he thought.

"Damn, I'll be glad to get back to the ranch," one of the men said. "I hope the chink's got breakfast ready. It's been so long since I et, my stomach thinks my throat's been cut."

"That can be arranged," Culhane growled.

"Aw, I didn't mean nothin' by it, boss. I'm just hungry, that's all."

"Just hush, Oswald," Culhane said wearily. He reined in his horse a little, dropping back to ride alongside Longarm.

There was enough light now for Longarm to be able to see the boss outlaw. Culhane was around thirty, Longarm judged, and good-looking with dark blond hair under a cream-colored Stetson. His range clothes were not flashy

92

or expensive, but they were good quality, as were his saddle, gunbelt, and spurs. Whatever had motivated Culhane to become a rustler, it wasn't poverty. The man's ranch must have been fairly successful.

But some folks were like that, thought Longarm. Plenty was never enough. Even if they went along for years, seemingly satisfied with their lives, greed and discontent were still festering in them, and sooner or later it came out. Longarm had no idea what had finally brought out the villainy in Culhane, and he didn't give a damn. It was enough that it was there.

"Look, my friend, I know you must be some sort of lawman," Culhane said. "Otherwise you wouldn't have started asking questions around Castleton about those train holdups. I knew when I heard about what you were doing that the smart thing would be to get rid of you before you had a chance to find out anything. But I want to know who you work for, so I'll know who to look out for in the future."

Longarm didn't say anything. Culhane's persistent questioning had given him a couple of points to mull over, however. Culhane had just admitted being responsible for that ambush attempt in Longarm's hotel room back in Castleton, a couple of nights earlier. How had he known that Longarm was poking around and asking questions about the rustling? Longarm had tried to remain inconspicuous when he arrived in Castleton, but he had talked to several people, including Sheriff Willard and Elizabeth. He knew neither of them could have tipped off Culhane. There was the hotel clerk, and old Alf, the hostler at Elizabeth's livery stable. Longarm didn't recall saying anything to either of them that would have made them overly suspicious of him if they were working for Culhane, but he supposed it was possible. Or maybe Culhane had instructed his agent in Castleton to report any stranger who showed up, because there probably weren't that many.

The fact that Longarm could have been seen talking to the sheriff might have been enough to cause Culhane to order the bushwhack attempt.

Culhane's determination to find out who Longarm worked for told the big lawman something else. He was sure that Culhane or one of the other outlaws must have searched his pockets after he was knocked out. If the little leather folder containing his badge and bona fides had been in his pocket, as it had been when he left Castleton, they would have found it. That meant the identification had slipped out of his pocket at one time or another, quite possibly while he was inside that well. The leather folder could be on the bottom of the well, along with his hat.

Both items could be replaced, Longarm told himself. If it even mattered. If he lived long enough.

"Look, fella," Culhane went on. "I've got an old Chinese cook on my spread. He used to work for one of those warlords over in China, and he learned enough ways to make a man suffer that he could put an Apache to shame when it comes to torture. I don't want to turn him loose on you, but I will if you don't tell me what I want to know."

For the first time, Longarm spoke. "And if I . . . tell you?"

"I'll have my cook patch up that bullet wound instead, and you'll stay on my ranch for a while. As my guest."

Longarm didn't believe that for a second. He just grunted in disdain.

"No, I mean it," Culhane said, correctly interpreting Longarm's reaction. "You don't have any way of knowing this, mister, but I've got some other things to be concerned with right now, more important things than being annoyed by somebody like you. Whether you live or die doesn't mean a hill of beans to me. If I find out you're not a threat to me, I don't have to kill you, just keep you locked up for a while."

Culhane sounded sincere, but Longarm knew better than to believe him. Still, he was curious enough to say, "If I tell you what you want to hear, how will you know it's the truth?"

Culhane grinned. "Well, I might have to let Cookie work on you a little, just to make sure you're in the right mood to be telling the truth. But I can promise you, it won't be nearly as bad if you cooperate."

Longarm grunted again. He still believed that Culhane would kill him as soon as he was convinced that Longarm hadn't told anyone else about the wells in the desert. Especially after all the talk that gave away the fact Culhane was really a rancher over around Bell City.

The sun was up now, and Longarm could see the Solomons plainly. He could even see the band of green along the base of the mountains that marked the rangeland. What he couldn't see was any way to escape from Culhane and the other rustlers.

The horse he was riding must have belonged to one of the men he had killed. He looked around, saw a couple of bodies roped over the back of a single horse. Several other men had bloodstained bandages wrapped around arms or legs or shoulders, telling Longarm that his shots had done some damage. The wounded men glared at him, and he knew he couldn't expect any mercy from them. Just as he had thought earlier, mercy would come in the form of a quick death, if it came at all.

A sudden wind whipped up dust around the hooves of the horses, causing a few of them to shy nervously. Longarm's side hurt like hell, but he forced his brain to work anyway. Something about the light was different. It had taken on a more reddish hue in the past few minutes, he realized. The sun wasn't as warm as it usually was, either. Even this early in the morning, the heat should have been rising. Instead, Longarm felt a chill that he didn't think had anything to do with his loss of blood.

Culhane hipped around in the saddle, looked behind them, and said, "Shit." Something definitely was wrong. Longarm was still riding hunched over. He twisted his head as much as he could and saw that the sun had turned into a round orange ball as it climbed higher in the sky. It was well-defined, not the blinding glare that it usually was. The wind blew harder, picking up more dust and swirling it around the riders, all of whom were now looking back.

"Storm comin', boss," one of them said, putting into words what all of them knew, including Longarm.

"Blast it, we've still got a couple of miles to go before we're out of this damned desert," Culhane said.

"That dust is movin' fast," another man said. "If we don't get off the *Llano Caliente* before the worst of it gets here, we'll be in a fix for sure."

Culhane jerked his head in a nod. "Lewis, throw a loop over that bastard's saddle horn. You're responsible for keeping up with him."

Lewis was the rustler who had wanted to kill him earlier, Longarm recalled. Culhane could have picked somebody better to be responsible for getting him safely out of the desert before the sandstorm rolled over them. On the other hand, even a bloodthirsty son of a bitch like Lewis probably would think twice before crossing the leader of the gang.

Longarm coughed as the dust thickened in the air around him. He winced as the spasm made fresh agony jab into his bullet-gouged side. His hands tightened on the saddle horn.

Lewis spurred over beside him and said, "Move your hands." Longarm pulled them back as much as the bindings would allow, and Lewis worked the loop of a lariat over the horn and pulled it tight. He played out a few yards of the rope and then took a dally around his own saddle horn so that his horse and Longarm's would remain connected, even if the dust got too thick for them to see each other.

More than once over the years, Longarm had seen such storms come roaring like freight trains over various deserts. They were slow to develop, but once they did, they moved fast. It was unusual for one to strike this early in the day; usually they hit in the late afternoon. But it was not unheard of, and there was no denying the evidence. The sun had vanished now, its location marked by nothing more than a faint red glow. The blue of the sky still showed directly overhead, but it was being devoured by the second, swallowed up by the huge cloud of sand that was sweeping across the earth. The height of the towering cloud revealed just how strong the oncoming storm really was. It hurt Longarm to turn around and look, but he couldn't stop himself. The sandstorm was one hell of an impressive sight.

The rustlers whipped their horses into a run. Connected by the rope to Lewis's horse, Longarm's mount had no choice but to gallop along with the others. They were in a race now. If they could reach the edge of the desert before the dust cloud rolled over them, they would be relatively safe. They would still have to breath a lot of dust, but the rangeland and the mountains beyond would break the force of the storm. The rustlers could hunker down in some trees and wait out the big blow. Then, they could proceed to their original destination.

But if the storm caught them still on the *Llano Caliente,* they would be blinded and would run the risk of getting separated, turned around, and completely lost. They might even be buried beneath one of the shifting sand dunes. So there was a definite air of desperation about the group of riders as they dashed toward the edge of the desert.

After a few minutes, with the cloud looming more and more above them, Longarm knew they weren't going to make it. He could see the green rangeland up ahead, but it was still too far away. As the dust grew ever thicker, some of the men cursed and yelled angrily over the noise of the wind, which had risen into a mad howl.

But even knowing what was coming, Longarm wasn't fully prepared for the sheer violence of the storm when it finally struck.

The wind already was blowing hard, but it slammed into the men with a force many times greater than it had possessed only seconds earlier. Like a physical blow, it staggered the horses, and one of the luckless animals lost its footing and fell with a shrill, terrified whinny. None of the outlaws stopped to help the man whose horse had gone down. They galloped on, leaving him behind to try to get the maddened animal back on its feet.

Longarm held tight to the saddle horn of his mount. With his eyes slitted almost closed, he peered around. The blowing sand was so thick and blinding that the other riders were nothing but blurs to him now. He could still see Lewis fairly clearly, but that was all. Lewis had pulled his bandanna up over his mouth and nose to block some of the dust, but Longarm had no such protection. He coughed and wheezed and gagged. It was like trying to breathe underground.

Under the circumstances, there was no way the gang could stay together. Within minutes, no one could see more than a few feet in front of his face. Though battered and stung by the storm, Longarm knew it represented his best—no, his *only*—chance of escape. He forced all thoughts of anything else out of his mind and concentrated on what he was doing.

The bonds that fastened his hands to the saddle horn had enough play in them so that he could reach over and grasp the lariat Lewis had attached to the horn. Using his knees to guide his panicky mount, Longarm angled the horse toward Lewis's horse, taking in the slack of the rope as he did so. Only about a dozen feet separated them.

When the horse tried to pull back in the other direction, Longarm's iron grip on the rope prevented it from doing so.

He drew closer and closer to Lewis. The shape of the rustler and his horse became more distinct. Lewis wasn't paying any attention to Longarm. All he wanted to do was to get off the desert before he choked to death on the flying sand. He seemed not to realized Longarm was there until the horses were running alongside each other no more than three feet apart.

With a startled curse, Lewis reached for his gun. As his fingers clawed at the butt of the Colt on his hip, Longarm lashed out with the slack of the rope he had gathered up. The length of rope, doubled over thickly, cut across Lewis's face. He yelled in surprise, more startled than hurt, and the revolver slipped out of his fingers, dropping to the sand. Longarm slashed at the rustler again with the rope. Lewis threw up an arm to ward off the lariat, and the loop slipped around his arm, catching at the elbow.

Longarm swerved away suddenly, holding tight to the rope. With another scream, Lewis was jerked out of the saddle. Longarm played out a little rope but hung on grimly. Lewis was dragged across the sand between the two racing horses.

There were rocks here and there in the sand, Longarm knew. Lewis was being battered by them, but Longarm couldn't hear the thudding impacts over the roaring wind. All he knew was that no one could survive such an ordeal for long.

He had no idea where the other rustlers were. They could be five yards away or five hundred for all he knew. The only thing he could do was keep riding blindly ahead and hope for the best. The storm would blow itself out eventually. If he could hang on that long and not choke to death first, he had a chance.

For an unknowable time, everything in life boiled down

to a few simple objectives for Longarm. Stay in the sad-dle. Keep the horses moving. Don't let go of the rope. Those were the things he needed to do to stay alive. Somehow, for what seemed like an eternity, he managed to do them.

Gradually he became aware that the wind wasn't blowing as hard. There was still a lot of sand in the air, but not as much as before. The horses had slowed to a plodding, trudging gait, and as Longarm looked down, he saw something under their hooves that he had hoped, but not expected, to see again.

Grass.

He had reached the rangeland east of the Solomons. He was out of the *Llano Caliente*.

For minutes on end, Longarm slumped forward in the saddle, shaking with exhaustion and relief. His nose and mouth were clogged with sand, and his eyes were crusted almost closed. Snorting, coughing, and spitting, he cleared enough of the sand from his nose and mouth so that he was able to breathe a little easier, but he still couldn't see very well.

A rumble of thunder sounded in the distance. The storm had reached the mountains, and as the rocky slopes forced the air up, a storm of a different sort began to develop. Black clouds formed overhead, and jagged fingers of lightning clawed through them.

Longarm looked around. He didn't see any sign of the rustlers, but he knew his vision wasn't at its best right now. The only one of the outlaws he could see was Lewis, and Lewis no longer posed a threat. Being dragged across the desert in that wild race through the storm had shredded his clothes and battered his body. His head was particu-larly misshapen, pounded into something so grotesque that it barely seemed human. The arm that was caught in the rope had been jerked out of its socket and was barely hanging on to the shoulder by a few strands of meat and muscle. Longarm was glad the arm hadn't been torn off completely. If that had happened, Lewis's body would be lying somewhere out there in the desert, unable to help Longarm in any way.

Holding on to the saddle horn, Longarm worked his feet out of the stirrups and swung his right leg up and over the back of the horse. He was so weak he would have fallen if not for his grip on the horn and the cords binding him to it. He hung there for a moment, his feet back on the ground at last, his head leaned against the skirt of the saddle. Slowly, his quaking nerves and jerking muscles calmed down.

He turned his head to look at Lewis's corpse. The rustler's handgun was gone, dropped when Longarm slashed his face with the rope. There was no rifle hanging from Lewis's saddle, either. But he wore a knife sheathed on his left hip. Judging from the shape of the sheath, it was a bowie, Longarm decided.

Neither of the horses wanted to get any closer to the dead man than they had to. Longarm convinced his mount to approach Lewis by tugging on the saddle horn and talking to the animal in low, soothing tones. When he was close enough to reach the corpse with his foot, he used the toe of his boot to work the knife out of its sheath. Once he had the bowie free, he scooted it over to a small rock and used both feet to lift the blade and rest it on the rock, close to the grip. It was a clumsy process and required quite a bit of time. While Longarm was doing that, more thunder rumbled up in the mountains and more lightning flashed. He didn't know if it was going to rain down here where he was, but there would be a shower in the high country.

When he had the knife positioned the way he wanted it, he lifted his foot and brought his toe down sharply on the end of the blade, flipping the knife into the air. His hands lunged out the few inches they were allowed by their bindings. His fingers reached for the handle of the bowie. If he missed, either he wouldn't catch the knife or else he'd slice a couple of fingers off. In the first case, he could try again. In the second, he'd probably bleed to death before he could do anything about it.

He missed.

Longarm muttered a curse as the knife thudded to the ground. He had to start again, laboriously pushing and prodding and lifting with his booted toes, working the knife into place so that it was balanced on the rock. Then another stomp, and again the weapon spun up into the air.

It took him four attempts before his fingertips brushed the rawhide-wrapped handle of the knife. It was the seventh try before he was able to grab hold of it and hang on to it.

Longarm was trembling with weakness again, so hard that he was afraid he would drop the knife. With an effort of will, he forced his muscles to obey his commands. The position was awkward, but he was able to twist the knife around so that the edge of the blade was against the cords lashed to his wrists. Lewis kept a keen edge on his knife, Longarm had to give him that. In a few minutes' time, he was able to saw through the bindings and only nicked himself once. That was only a minor scratch.

The cords fell away from his wrists. He staggered a few steps away from the horse, free for what seemed like the first time in ages. Something hit him on top of the head. He looked up, and a raindrop splashed against his cheek. Another drop fell, fat and heavy, then another and another as the sky overhead opened up in a blinding downpour.

Longarm stood there laughing and crying as the rain sluiced off the sand that had coated his face so thickly he probably had looked like some sort of monster. He cupped his hands and let them fill with water and splashed it in his eyes, washing away the grit. His eyes burned and stung but as he blinked away the rain he found that he could see better. He danced up and down, ignoring the pain in his side. He was alive, damn it, alive!

Then, he heard the hoofbeats and knew he was alive but afoot, because the two horses had run off. Between the storm and the dead man, they were too spooked to stand there while Longarm capered around in the rain like a little kid or a madman.

He stopped his celebrating and looked around, and sure enough, both horses were gone. Still yoked together by the rope, they had had no choice but to stampede together. And when they left, they had taken Lewis's arm with them, ripping apart the slender strings of flesh that had attached it to his body.

So there he was, thought Longarm, alone, wounded, nearly weaponless, and on the far side of the *Llano Caliente* desert with a dead man—or what was left of one, anyway. Plus Culhane and the rest of that band of killers would be searching for him soon, if they weren't already. Given all that, it was a wonder that he could smile as he lurched away from Lewis's body and started walking through the rain.

But Longarm was grinning from ear to ear. He was alive!

Chapter 10

And Elizabeth Townsend was dead.

That thought came to Longarm when he had gone less than fifty yards. His elation at his own survival and his escape from the gang of rustlers vanished, to be replaced by a deep anger and melancholy. Culhane had a lot to answer for. Rustling was one thing, stealing the United States mail was another, and Longarm would have happily put the son of a bitch behind bars for either or both of those crimes. But the way Elizabeth had been shot down so callously, so brutally—that made it personal. Longarm was going to even the score with Culhane, no matter how long it took or how dangerous it might be.

Grim-faced now, Longarm stumbled on as the wind died down and the rain stopped. The sun stayed behind the clouds that had formed when the sandstorm reached the mountains, and that was a relief. Longarm was actually cool in his wet clothes, and that gave him a little strength. He didn't know how long he could keep going before all his reserves ran out, but he wanted to put some distance between himself and Culhane's men.

Of course, that was going to be sort of difficult to do, he reflected, when he didn't know where he was or where they were. But when he stood with his back to the desert and then turned left, he knew he was facing south. If he kept going that way long enough, he would reach Bell City sooner or later, or if Bell City was the other way, behind him, then he would come to Rossville, the railroad junction town. In either case, he ought to be able to get help. Sheriff Willard had said there was a lawman in Bell City—name of Hampton, or something like that, Longarm recalled—and there would certainly be one in Rossville, too. One thing he was certain of was that he didn't want to venture out into that desert again anytime soon, not if he could avoid it.

Exhausted, wounded, he found himself slipping in and out of a daze as he walked. In his more coherent moments, he studied his surroundings. The rangeland here was not as good as it was over in Rampart Valley. The grass was sparser and the ground was dotted with clusters of rocks. Here, in what amounted to the foothills of the Solomon Mountains, there were rugged ridges that thrust up suddenly and gullies that were choked with thick brush. Still, it wasn't the worst land for ranching that Longarm had ever seen. With a lot of work and some hardy stock, a cattleman could make a go of it around here. That must be what Culhane had done. But Culhane had grown tired of the work and decided to improve his stock by adding to it from the herds of other men, herds that had been stolen from Rampart Valley and driven across the desert.

Longarm came to a creek, a tiny, fast-flowing trickle that ran down out of the mountains and twisted through the rangeland on its way to the desert, where it likely was soaked up in a hurry by the thirsty sands. He went to his knees, cupped a shaking hand in the stream, and lifted the water to his mouth. It tasted wonderful, so delicious that with a groan Longarm lowered himself full length on the ground and plunged his head into the creek. The water was cold and clear and bracing. When he finally lifted his mouth from it, he felt like he had sucked down a gallon.

He intended to lie there only for a moment with his head pillowed on his arms, but before he knew what was happening, he was sound asleep.

The sound of a shot woke Longarm. His head jerked up from where it lay on his arms, and he looked around wildly, unsure of what had disturbed him and how long he had been asleep. Then he heard the distant blast of a rifle and figured another shot had jolted him out of his exhausted slumber. A good thing, too, because he couldn't afford to lollygag around while a bunch of killers were after him. Those shots might not have anything to do with Culhane and his men, but on the other hand, it was possible they were the ones doing the shooting.

Longarm pushed himself onto hands and knees. His arms and legs tried to fold up underneath him, but he stiffened his muscles and forced them to accept his weight. He looked around, saw a small tree a few yards away, and crawled over to it. Clinging to the tree, he pulled himself up until he was standing shakily on his feet.

The clouds overhead were breaking up. The storm of the morning was nothing more than a distant memory now. Longarm checked the position of the sun, saw to his dismay that it was past its zenith. He had lain there next to the creek, senseless, for hours. The day was more than half gone.

He took a few minutes to orient himself and then started walking south again. Instead of strengthening him, the rest seemed to have made him even weaker. He could barely put one foot in front of the other. He was light-headed, too, so much so that at times it seemed as if his head was about to detach itself from his body and float away on the hot breeze that swept from the desert over the rangeland.

His clothes had dried by now. He expected them to

grow wet with sweat as the sunlight poured down through the gaps in the clouds and baked him with its heat. He didn't seem to be sweating, though. Something about that worried Longarm.

He became even more worried when a strong chill suddenly gripped him and made him shiver. It passed in a few minutes, but it left him even weaker than before.

His shirt was plastered by dried blood to his side where the bullet had ripped its way in and out of his body. He paused and slipped his left hand inside his shirt, reaching over to explore the area around the wound as best he could. The flesh there seemed swollen, and it was scalding hot to the touch. The bullet hole was festering. Corruption had gotten into it, and it would kill him if he didn't get some help.

Longarm stumbled ahead again, muttering to himself. He had no idea how far it was to the nearest town. Maybe he could find a ranch somewhere closer.

But Culhane had a ranch over here somewhere, he reminded himself. Wouldn't that be rich, if he waltzed right up to the ranch house of the man who was looking for him and wanted to kill him?

No, he had to avoid ranches, he told himself. He had to get to a town, either Bell City or Rossville.

Movement up ahead caught his eye and made him lurch into a small grove of trees. He wanted to hide until he could tell who was up there. As he leaned against a tree trunk and watched through the brush, he caught sight of some cattle ambling along through a pasture. That was what he had seen, he decided after a few minutes. He watched close, to make sure no cowboy was hazing the stock along, but the cattle were moving on their own, more than likely looking for some better graze. Longarm came out of hiding and stumbled on. When he passed the cattle, he could see they were branded with a Circle C.

Time passed without him being aware of it. When he

finally looked at the sun again, he was startled to see how low to the horizon it was. Night would be coming on before much longer. He stopped, rubbed a hand over his face. How long had it been since he'd eaten? He had no idea. The chills were coming more often now, shaking him to his core. But when he touched his forehead, it was blistering. How could he be so hot and so cold at the same time?

He knew he was in the grip of a raging fever. He couldn't keep going much longer. He had to have help . . .

"Don't move, you big son of a bitch! Stand right there, or I'll ventilate you!"

The excited, angry voice came from behind Longarm. He stopped, his arms hanging loosely at his sides. He was mildly curious who had found him, but turning around to look would have been just too much of a chore. The voice was a little familiar, though.

A moment later his captor came into view, holding the reins of the horse he was leading with one hand and using the other hand to brandish a revolver at Longarm, who recognized him as one of Culhane's gang. "Where's Lewis, you bastard?" the rustler demanded. "What'd you do with him?"

Longarm didn't answer for a moment. His mouth was too dry to form words. Finally he was able to swallow a little, and he said, "We ain't . . . traveling together anymore."

The outlaw looked at the bowie knife tucked behind Longarm's belt. "That's Lewis's knife!" he exclaimed. He dropped his horse's reins, yanked out the knife, and shook it at Longarm. "You killed him, didn't you? I don't know how you managed it, but you killed him!"

"The desert . . . killed him."

"Yeah, well, I wish the desert had killed you! We all thought it was a mistake to keep you alive, but Culhane said we had to until you'd talked." The man lifted the

Colt in his hand and pointed it at Longarm's face. The muzzle of the gun looked as big around as the mouth of a cannon. "I oughta put a bullet between your eyes right now for what you did to Lewis!"

"If you do that," Longarm rasped, "you won't be able to collect a payoff from Culhane."

The outlaw blinked in surprise. "How'd you know about that? Culhane didn't offer us a bonus for findin' you until after you'd escaped."

"Just seemed like . . . the kind of thing Culhane would do."

"You've got him figured pretty good, mister." The outlaw slipped the bowie behind his own belt, then jerked the gun in his other hand. "Now come on. I'm takin' you back to the ranch."

"I can't . . . walk any farther. I'm hurt."

"Huh! Don't expect no sympathy from me. You can still talk with bullets through both knees. I'll throw a rope around you and drag you if I have to."

Longarm knew the man meant the threat. He didn't look overly smart, but he had a vicious cunning in his little piggish eyes. Longarm asked, "Which . . . way?"

"Over thataway," the outlaw said, pointing with the Colt in his hand.

Longarm turned to the west and took a step, then let out a groan and fell to his knees. He swayed back and forth as if he were about to topple over.

The outlaw swore, jammed his gun back in its holster, and took a step toward Longarm. "Damn it, get up—"

Longarm threw himself at the man's knees. Everything around him was distorted, and he couldn't tell if he was moving fast or slow. But he must have been fast enough to take the outlaw by surprise, because he crashed into the man's legs. Longarm grabbed on tight and heaved, and the outlaw went over backward with a startled yelp.

Longarm drew on the last of his reserves and smashed

a fist into the man's groin. The outlaw had been clawing at the butt of his gun, but the blow made him cry out in pain and double over on the ground. Longarm's hand closed around the handle of the bowie knife. There was no time to try to take the weapon away from the outlaw. Instead, Longarm yanked up on the handle, twisted the blade, and plunged it into the man's abdomen.

The outlaw screamed this time. Longarm held tight to the knife, burying it as deep in the man's guts as he could. The outlaw fumbled his gun out of its holster, but it fell from his fingers before he could fire. Longarm twisted the knife again. His fingers were slick with blood now.

The outlaw's back arched up off the ground, then he fell back, suddenly going limp all over. Longarm collapsed on top of the man's body, lying there and feeling the quiver of death that went through the outlaw as a final breath rattled in the man's throat. Then everything was silent and still once more.

Longarm was trembling, too. The exertion of fighting for his life had been almost too much for him. His side was wet with fresh blood where the wound had broken open. He felt himself about to pass out and clung grimly to consciousness. After a few minutes, he was able to push himself off the corpse.

He pulled the bowie knife from the outlaw's ripped-open guts and wiped it clean on the grass. Then, he picked up the dead man's Colt. Longarm was still wearing his own holster. He slipped the gun into the cross-draw rig. He climbed to his feet, taking his time. He had no choice in the matter. He had to stop to rest every few seconds.

A look around told him that the outlaw's horse had run off. Longarm heard a dry, hollow rattle, sort of like the sound a mesquite pod makes when the wind makes the beans roll around inside it, and, after a moment, he realized he was laughing. He wasn't able to keep a horse these days. They all ran away from him as soon as they got the chance.

The sun was setting. Longarm kept it on his left and set out again, finding the strength somehow to keep walking. He left the dead outlaw behind him. Culhane might find the corpse, and if he did, he would know that Longarm was out here somewhere, alive and on the loose. That meant Longarm couldn't afford to rest, no matter how tired he was. The task now facing him was the same as it had been all day. He had to find the town before Culhane found him.

But at least now he had a gun again. The weight of the Colt felt good on his hip, even though it was a few more pounds for his exhausted muscles to carry.

The sun sank below the Solomon Mountains. Darkness fell quickly. Longarm welcomed the night. It would make him harder to find. But as soon as the sun was gone, the freezing cold set in. The night wasn't really that frigid, he knew. The fever was causing what he felt, at least most of it. His blood was carrying poison from the infected wound through his veins, and though his body was trying to fight back, he had a feeling this was one fight he couldn't win. He wondered if he would be alive when the sun came up in the morning.

He was alive, all right. That was surprising enough in itself. But what was really surprising, he thought as he stared in consternation at the screaming woman across the room, was where he had woken up.

And what she had been doing to him.

She was a good-looking young woman with thick blond hair falling around a tanned, lightly freckled face. The dress she wore revealed a body that was slender but curved in all the right places. She stopped screaming and started to raise her hands to her face, but she halted the gesture as she looked at her fingers and saw they were

111

slick with the seed she had just milked out of his still-stiff organ. Her eyes went back and forth between Long-arm and her hands, staring in horror. She had jumped away from him like a terrified deer a moment earlier, as if she'd just realized what she was doing.

Longarm's tongue came out, feeling like a dried husk, and scraped over equally dry lips. "Ma'am," he managed to say, "don't be scared. I ain't goin' to . . . hurt you . . ."

He was so weak and dizzy he wouldn't have represented much of a threat to a newborn kitten, let alone an obviously healthy and vital young woman. His head sank back against the pillow and his eyes closed. The eyelids felt like they weighed a ton apiece. A long, ragged sigh came from his lips.

After a moment, something cool touched his forehead, bringing with it blessed relief. He heard himself groaning. Prying open his eyes, he saw that the woman had come back to the bed and laid a wet cloth on his forehead. "You've got a fever," she said. "That wound in your side is probably infected."

"Yes, ma'am," Longarm whispered. That was all the strength he had. "I . . . expect so."

"You wait right here. I'll fetch the doctor."

The corners of Longarm's mouth lifted in what passed for a smile. "Don't reckon I'll be . . . running off . . . anytime soon."

"Dobie, you keep an eye on our guest."

Longarm wondered who Dobie was. But then the woman snapped her fingers, and a small black and brown and tan dog with big ears and a pointed noise hopped up onto the foot of the bed and sat down. The dog solemnly regarded Longarm with large, intelligent eyes.

"I'll be right back with Doc Barkley," the woman went on.

"Ma'am?"

Longarm's weak voice stopped her as she started to

112

turn away. She looked back and said, "Yes?"

"I'm . . . much obliged . . . for everything."

Her eyes darted toward his groin, where his long, thick shaft, gone soft now, lay along his abdomen. She touched her lips with her tongue and looked away hurriedly, but not before Longarm saw the look of shame and confusion that passed across her face. He hadn't meant what she thought he did. But there was no denying what had happened between them.

"I'll be back," she said again, and this time, when she went to the door, he let her go.

Longarm closed his eyes and rested again, expecting to fall asleep. He didn't, though. His mind remained awake and at least partially alert. The memories of everything that had happened in the past two days were strong in him. He recalled walking on through the night for what seemed like hours after killing the rustler and taking his gun. The bleeding in his side had slowed, but not stopped. The fever made him crazy for a while, and he saw things—phantasms, monsters, ghosts from his past—that he didn't want to think about too much.

And then he had seen the lights up ahead, warm yellow glows floating in the darkness. At first he had believed them to be illusions, too, but finally he had convinced himself they were real and walked toward them. The lights were from houses in either Bell City or Rossville, he didn't know which. And it didn't matter. He would find someone to help him, and maybe he would live after all. For a lot of years, he had been damned hard to kill, and he wanted to maintain that record.

To his incredible frustration, however, he had collapsed and passed out just before reaching one of the lights. He had remained mired in oblivion for an unknown time, rousing only when a sharp, persistent sound finally penetrated his brain. Now he opened his eyes, looked at the dog curled up on the foot of the bed, and said, "I reckon that was you . . . barking at me, Dobie."

The dog's ears perked up at the mention of his name, but he didn't get to his feet. Longarm closed his eyes again. He remembered climbing with difficulty to an upright position, leaning on some sort of shed, and then a woman's voice had spoken to him. After that, everything was a blank. But he could make a few guesses and piece together what had happened. The young woman had come out of her house to investigate the barking and found him. When he passed out, she had gotten him in the house some way and put him to bed. While he was unconscious, he had dreamed that he was making love to Elizabeth Townsend, and the blonde, whatever her name was, had seen the evidence of his arousal and helped him to a climax. He wasn't sure why she would have done such a thing, and from the look on her face right afterward, she was just as shocked as he was. Probably more so.

Was she alone here in the house, except for the dog? That seemed likely. She hadn't mentioned anyone else being around, and he hadn't heard anybody moving inside the house since she left.

She had said she was going to fetch a doctor for him. When she got back with the sawbones, he would ask her to bring the local lawman, too. The sooner Longarm got to talk to a fellow star packer, the better.

He had quite a story to tell . . . about stolen cattle, and wells dynamited out of the desert sands, and a cold-blooded killer named Culhane.

Chapter 11

It was late enough now so that quite a few people were moving around on the main street of Bell City. Sarah Hodge hurried along the street toward Doc Barkley's office. She was distracted, and she barely heard the greetings given her by some of the townspeople she passed. She forced her attention back on what she was doing, made herself smile and nod pleasantly. But it was hard not to dwell on the bizarre events of the morning so far.

Finding a stranger with a gunshot wound in her back yard was bad enough. Whatever had possessed her to . . . to do the other thing she had done? And on today, of all days! Her brain burned with shame and regret. Brent would never forgive her.

If he knew about it. Maybe the best thing to do would be to never tell him everything that had happened. Finding an injured stranger and helping him, that was one thing. That was just being a Good Samaritan. No one could find fault with that, least of all Brent. She just wouldn't mention any of the other details, Sarah decided.

But could she do that? Could she conceal the truth from the man she loved? Was that any way to start their life together, with a lie of omission between them?

She glanced down at her hands. They had been stained with blood and . . . other things . . . but she had cleaned them off so that no sign remained of what had happened. They wouldn't give her away. No one knew the details except her and the mysterious stranger. If he was a gentleman—and something about him told Sarah that he was, despite his rugged appearance—he would keep that knowledge to himself.

But would lying just make things worse in the long run? Would Brent be less likely to forgive her for hiding the truth than he would be for giving in to her baser impulses?

A part of her brain suddenly insisted there had been nothing base about what she had done. She was just trying to bring some relief to a suffering man, that was all. What she had done was . . . medicinal, that was it. Like a teetotaler taking a slug of whiskey to relieve the suffering of an illness or an injury.

She had to keep on telling herself that, she thought. If she did, she might come to believe it sooner or later.

Dr. Winslow Barkley's office and living quarters were on the second floor of a large frame building, above Carlson's General Mercantile Store. Sarah reached the flight of outside stairs that led up to the landing just outside the doctor's office. She hoped Barkley was here this morning and not off tending to a patient at some isolated ranch or mining claim in the mountains.

Her footsteps rang on the steps as she climbed to the landing. Barkley must have heard her coming, because he opened the door even before she got there. As she reached the landing, the medico looked out at her in surprise and said, "Sarah? What's wrong? I'd have thought you'd be home getting ready for this afternoon."

Barkley was in his late fifties, a medium-sized man with a mostly bald head and a perpetually dour expression. He was a good doctor, though, and had been attending to the sick of Bell City and the surrounding rangeland for well over a decade. He was in his shirtsleeves this morning, wiping his hands on a towel after washing up.

Sarah was a little breathless from hurrying along the street and up the stairs. "Doctor, there's a man . . . a man at my house," she said. "He's been hurt."

"A man?" Barkley repeated. "A man, you say? What man? Who is he?"

Sarah shook her head. "I don't know. I never saw him before. But it looks like he's been shot in the side, and I think the wound must be infected. He's hot, like he has a fever."

"Good Lord! You don't know who he is, you say?"

"No, not at all."

Barkley tossed the towel aside. "Well, it doesn't really matter, does it? A wounded man is a wounded man. Let me get my hat and coat, and my bag . . ." He turned and hurried back into his office.

A couple of minutes later, he and Sarah were walking down the street toward Sarah's house on the outskirts of town. Barkley had jammed a bowler hat on his head, and he wore a grimly purposeful expression on his face. Despite the fact that she was an inch or so taller than him, Sarah had to hurry a little to keep up. She waved distractedly to one of the ladies of the town who smiled at her and said, "Today is the big day, isn't it, Sarah?"

It was a big day, all right, but she couldn't allow herself to think about that now. Not until she had dealt with the fact that she had a strange man in her bed, a man with at least one bullet hole in him.

As the two of them entered the house a few minutes later, Dobie barked and came running from the bedroom. Doc Barkley stepped past the little dog, who capered around Sarah's feet. She ignored him, too, and followed Barkley into the bedroom.

The stranger was awake. He looked at Barkley and said

117

in a weak voice, "You must be . . . the sawbones."

"That's right. Dr. Winslow Barkley. And who are you, my good man?"

"Name's Long . . . Custis Long."

To her great relief, Sarah saw that Custis Long had pulled part of the blanket over him, so that his lower half was covered. She had been in such a hurry to get out of here earlier that she'd gone off and left him with his . . . organ . . . hanging out of his long underwear.

The doctor placed his bag on a small table beside the bed, opened it, and took out a small pair of scissors. Hovering over the bed, he got to work immediately, cutting away the injured man's jacket and shirt around the wound. He sniffed and said, "Festering, all right. I can smell it. You're lucky to still be alive, young man."

"Reckon I . . . know that, Doc," Custis Long said.

"It won't be pleasant getting what's left of that shirt off the wound. It's stuck on there pretty good by all that dried blood."

"Do what you . . . got to do."

"Oh, I intend to. Sarah, I need some hot water—plenty of it. Can you tend to that?"

"Of course, Doctor," she said. To tell the truth, she was glad of the excuse to get out of the bedroom. She hurried to the kitchen, Dobie following at her heels, and started a fire in the stove.

By the time half an hour had passed, Dr. Barkley had used the hot water to soak loose the bits of fabric from the injured man's shirt that were stuck to the entrance wound. The exit wound was only a couple of inches farther back on the man's side, and it was cleaner. The bullet had plowed a tunnel through the man's flesh but seemed to have missed any bones or vital organs. A couple of inches one way and it would have missed him entirely; a couple of inches the other way and it would have killed him. As it was, the wound was messy and dangerous be-

118

cause of the amount of blood loss it had caused, not to mention the infection, but if those two things could be overcome, the wounded stranger stood a good chance of making a complete recovery.

Barkley explained all that to Custis Long and to Sarah as he cleaned the wounds. Long winced and gritted his teeth as the doctor swabbed out the holes with carbolic acid. "I apologize for the discomfort," Barkley said.

" 'Sallright, Doc," Long said. "I recollect once when I had to break open a few cartridges, pour the powder in a bullet hole, and set it off."

"Yes, that would certainly cauterize a wound, if one could stand the pain." Barkley looked over Long's torso, which was bared now. "You appear to have been wounded on quite a few different occasions, judging by those scars. And knifed as well." He pointed to a particular scar. "I'm not sure about that one. What caused it?"

"Lemme think," Long said. "An arrow, maybe. Tell you the truth, I disremember."

"Good Lord," Barkley muttered. "Man's been wounded so many times he can't keep up with them all, he says. You've led a dangerous life, my friend."

"I reckon so. Am I going to survive it a mite longer?"

"If I have anything to say about it," Barkley replied. "I have some moss in my bag that's proved effective in helping to heal bullet wounds. I'm going to pack some in those bullet holes and bind them up. Then it'll just be a matter of getting plenty of rest." He glanced at Sarah, who stood by watching with a solemn expression on her face. "But you'll have to do that elsewhere. You can't stay here."

"Why not?" Long asked.

"Because this girl's getting married this afternoon, that's why not!"

"Married," Longarm repeated. "I didn't have no idea."

119

The doctor sniffed. "Don't see how you would have, since you're not from around these parts. It'll be the biggest celebration we've had in Bell City for a while, though."

"That's where this is? Bell City?"

Barkley frowned at Longarm. "Don't you know where you are? Are you addled?"

"Just didn't know . . . if this was Bell City . . . or Rossville." Longarm summoned up a grin. "I'm a mite lost. First time I been on . . . this side of the *Llano Caliente*."

The woman leaned forward. "You came across the desert? On foot?"

"And wounded that way?" Barkley added.

"I wasn't on foot . . . the whole time. Didn't pick up this wound right away . . . either."

Barkley shook his head. "That wasteland is a bad place. It's claimed more than its share of lives over the years. I repeat, you're a lucky man, my friend."

"Is there a . . . lawman around here?" Longarm asked.

"I take it you want to report the attack that left you wounded." Barkley continued to work while he talked. "Once I'm done bandaging these wounds, Sarah can stay with you while I go get Sheriff Hampton. But then we'll have to see about moving you to my office. I think you can stand the trip. It won't take long."

Longarm nodded. "Sounds all right to me. I'm much obliged . . . to both of you."

Within a few more minutes, Barkley had finished wrapping strips of clean bandage around Longarm's torso. Sarah had to move to Longarm's side and help him sit up in bed as the doctor wrapped and tied off the dressings. Her hands were warm on the flesh of his arm as she gripped it, soft and yet strong at the same time. He glanced over at her, but she wouldn't meet his eyes.

When Barkley was finished, he put away the tools of

his trade and closed his bag. He took hold of Longarm's other arm, and between him and Sarah, they eased the big lawman back down to a resting position in the bed. "Stay right there," he said.

"I expect I will, Doc," Longarm replied with a smile.

Barkley grunted and looked at the young woman. "You might get him something to drink, Sarah. Water or maybe some broth. No coffee just yet. He doesn't need any stimulants."

"All right," she said. "What about something to eat?"

"Not just yet. Maybe later today, when the patient is stronger."

The young woman nodded. Longarm thought she looked nervous, and he figured he knew why she felt that way.

When the doctor was gone, the woman moved to the doorway of the bedroom and paused there, looking back at Longarm. He said, "You wish the doc had stayed here and sent you to get the sheriff, don't you, ma'am?"

"No, it's all right," she said, but she didn't sound too convincing. "I . . . I'll go fix you that broth. You can call if you need me. I'll hear you. It's not far to the kitchen."

Longarm nodded. "All right. And, ma'am . . . ? I am much obliged that you fetched me in here and went to get the doctor." He took care to be specific this time about expressing his gratitude. "Some folks would've left me laying out there on the ground."

"I couldn't do that," she said quickly. "You were hurt. You needed help."

"Well, I thank you, Sarah." He thought that was what the doctor had called her. "What other name goes with that?"

For a second he thought she wasn't going to tell him. Then she said, "Hodge. My name is Sarah Hodge."

"And this is your wedding day."

"That's right."

"I reckon you'll make a mighty pretty bride, Miss Hodge."

She looked down at the floor, clearly uncomfortable at being complimented. "Thank you," she said. She started to turn away.

Longarm stopped her one more time. "And if I said or did anything I shouldn't have while I was out of my head, ma'am, I'm sure sorry. When a fella's been shot and he's running a fever, well, he's liable not to think straight. Best just to act like anything he says or does didn't even happen."

He saw the expression of relief flicker across her face, saw as well the gratitude shining in her eyes as she looked at him. "That's all right, Mr. Long," she said. "If anything happened, it's already forgotten."

"Yes, ma'am."

He closed his eyes to rest as she left the room. He was lucky, all right. He could have died a dozen times over during the past two days, or at least it seemed like it. But he had survived, and now all he had to do was lie here and wait for the sheriff to arrive. Then he'd tell the local lawman his story. If there was a telegraph office in Bell City, the sheriff could send a wire directly to Billy Vail. If not, he'd have to send a rider down to Rossville. There would be a telegraph there for sure, since it was a railroad junction. In either case, help would be on the way before much longer.

He wondered if Culhane would be able to track him here to Sarah Hodge's house. Longarm hoped not. The last thing he wanted to do was to bring trouble down on her head after everything she had done to help him.

Just how desperate would Culhane be to get his hands on him? Would the boss outlaw risk riding into town and searching for him? He figured that Culhane was masquerading as a legitimate rancher, and that pose would be ruined if he and his men came in with guns drawn and started tearing the town apart. But if he allowed Longarm to live, the jig was up anyway. Longarm looked over at the table where Sarah had placed his coiled gunbelt and holster. He reached over, but his fingers couldn't quite grasp the butt of the Colt. When she came back, he would ask her to move the weapon a little closer. He didn't want to alarm her or anything, but the possibility of trouble from Culhane still existed.

Dobie ran into the room first and jumped on the bed, alerting Longarm to the fact that Sarah was coming back. She appeared in the doorway a moment later, carrying a tray with a bowl on it. Steam rose from the bowl. Longarm caught a whiff of a delicious aroma, and his stomach clenched in response, reminding him how long it had been since he'd eaten. He felt like his backbone was about to start poking out the front of his belly.

"That smells mighty good, ma'am," he said.

"It's just some beef broth, like the doctor suggested." Sarah brought the tray over to the bed and set it on the table next to the gun. "Can you sit up if I help you?"

"I reckon."

Again those warm, strong hands touched him, helping him into a sitting position. She propped a pillow behind him, then pulled a chair closer to the bed. "I'll feed you," she said as she sat down and took the tray on her lap.

Longarm wanted to tell her that she didn't have to go to that much bother, but to tell the truth, he still felt pretty shaky. Probably it would be a good idea for her to handle the spoon; otherwise he was liable to spill broth all over himself and the bed.

The broth tasted as good as it smelled. Longarm was dehydrated and half-starved, and if he could have, he would have grabbed hold of the bowl and guzzled down its contents in a couple of huge swallows. He forced himself to be patient as Sarah spooned the broth into his mouth. He could feel some of his strength coming back as she fed him. He had always had an iron constitution, and given the chance, he recovered quickly from most injuries.

As he ate, Longarm said, "I'm sure sorry to intrude on your wedding day like this, Miss Hodge. Reckon the doc's right that I'd be better off at his office. If you're getting married, you got plenty on your plate without having to worry about a shot-up pilgrim."

"That's all right, Mr. Long. I still have plenty of time to get ready. The ceremony isn't until five o'clock this afternoon."

"Big doin's, huh? The whole town will be there?" If that was the case, it might give Culhane and his men a chance to search the town without disturbing the citizens.

"The church should be packed," Sarah replied.

Something about her tone made Longarm look at her curiously. "Begging your pardon, ma'am," he said, "but you don't sound like you're too happy about that."

"Oh, I am, of course," she said quickly. "I love Brent. He's my fiancé. I just . . . well, I don't like crowds that much. The town's going to make a big fuss over us, and that just doesn't seem necessary. But I can't deny all my father's friends the chance to give us a big send-off into married life."

"What's your pa got to do with it?"

"He founded Bell City. He was the first mayor . . . the only mayor the town had until he passed away a couple of years ago."

"I'm sorry to hear about your loss."

Sarah put the spoon back in the empty bowl. "It was difficult for everyone to accept that he was gone. Everyone loved him. He was the only parent I ever knew. My mother died when I was born."

Longarm was struck by the similarity between Sarah's story and Elizabeth Townsend's life. It was almost like they could have been sisters. But Elizabeth's father was still alive—and Elizabeth wasn't. That thought made his mouth tighten into a hard, bitter line.

Sarah saw the reaction. "What's wrong?" she asked. "Is the broth bothering you?"

Longarm shook his head and said, "No, it was mighty good. I feel a heap better already. I was just . . . remembering something."

"Oh. About how you got shot, I imagine. I don't blame you for being upset about it. Would you like to tell me about it?"

"No, thanks. I reckon I'll wait until the doc gets here with the sheriff, so I'll only have to go through it once."

Sarah stood up. "Of course. I know you must be very tired. I'm sure Dr. Barkley will be back soon with Sheriff Hampton, but why don't you rest until they get here?"

"I might just do that."

"But I'll be close by if you need me," Sarah said. "Call out if you need anything."

"I'll be fine," Longarm assured her. "You'd best go on about your business. I imagine you've got a lot to do before the wedding."

"Yes, I suppose so." Sarah hesitated, then smiled ruefully and said, "You know, it's really hard to believe that by a little after five o'clock this afternoon, I'll be Mrs. Brent Culhane."

Chapter 12

With an effort, Longarm controlled the shock he felt and
didn't let it show on his face. Hoping that his voice
sounded normal he said, "That's your fella's name? Brent
Culhane?"

"That's right. You don't know him, do you?"

Longarm shook his head. "Nope. Lives here in town,
does he?"

"Oh, no, he has a ranch north of here. The Circle C.
You might have heard of it."

"Seems like I have," Longarm murmured, remembering
the brand on those cows he had seen the day before.
"Been around these parts for long?"

"About three years, I guess. Are you sure you don't
know him?"

"Well, maybe if you tell me what he looks like . . ."

"He's a little older than me, of course. I believe he's
twenty-nine." Sarah smiled. "And he's very handsome,
with dark blond hair. We'll have beautiful children together." She blushed as she made that last comment.

Longarm felt hollow inside, and this time it didn't have
anything to do with his wound or the other hardships he
had suffered. There was no doubt in his mind now that

Brent Culhane, the rancher who was going to marry Sarah Hodge later that day, was the same Culhane who had been raising hell over in Rampart Valley as the leader of a murderous gang of rustlers. He had to be sure, though.

"Seems like I knew a man named Culhane once. Any others around here by that name?"

Sarah shook her head. "None that I know of." She hefted the tray with the empty bowl on it. "I have to put this away now. Let me know if you need anything."

"Sure thing."

She left the room, and Longarm leaned his head back against the pillow propped behind him and heaved a deep sigh. What the hell was he going to do now? It was possible that Sarah Hodge had saved his life. At the very least, she had been an enormous help to him. How could he tell her that the man she was fixing to marry was a cold-blooded, murdering widelooper? How could he *not* tell her? He couldn't allow her to go through with the wedding, couldn't let her marry Culhane.

Doc Barkley seemed to know her pretty well. When the doc got back with Sheriff Hampton, Longarm would have to talk to the two men alone, without Sarah in the room. Then, he could explain who he was and how he came to be in Bell City. More importantly, he could explain about Culhane and why Sarah couldn't marry him. Barkley and Hampton would have to break the news to her. Better them than him.

So Culhane planned to get married this afternoon, Longarm mused. That meant he would show up at the church, probably with the rest of the gang on hand as well. The other rustlers would be the punchers on Culhane's ranch. Longarm had thought there was something different about the first member of the gang he had killed. These outlaws had a home: the Circle C ranch. They weren't drifting owlhoots, constantly on the dodge. No wonder the man hadn't been as ragged and dirty as the usual desperado.

For a few moments, Longarm toyed with the idea of asking Sheriff Hampton to arrest Culhane when he arrived at the church for the wedding. But that would never work, he realized. Culhane's men would be with him. Even with some deputies to back him up, the local lawman would be badly outnumbered. Once Barkley and Hampton had talked to Sarah, they would have to put their heads together and come up with some reason for postponing the ceremony that wouldn't tip off Culhane to the fact that his real identity had been exposed. Sarah had to string him along for a while, until a whole posse of deputy U.S. marshals could get to Bell City.

And, Longarm told himself, all that was assuming he could convince Barkley and Hampton of the truth, and they could convince Sarah. There was no guarantee of that, especially the latter. If Sarah thought highly enough of Culhane to marry him, it wouldn't be easy to make her believe that he was an outlaw.

He asked himself suddenly if maybe she already knew. Maybe she was in on the whole scheme. Then, with a curt shake of his head, he discarded the notion. It wasn't because she was beautiful that he refused to believe such a thing about her. He had run across plenty of damned good-looking women who were as crooked as a dog's hind leg. Some of them had been killers every bit as cold-blooded as Culhane. But he had seen the kindness and concern in Sarah Hodge's eyes, and he just didn't think she could ever sink so low as to be part of Culhane's plot. Longarm wasn't sure how Culhane planned to keep her in the dark once they were married, but he supposed it could be done. There were plenty of wives in the world who didn't know a blasted thing about their husband's business dealings.

After he'd spent some time thinking but not coming up

with any good answers for the dilemmas facing him, Longarm had a hankering for a cheroot. He didn't know if he had any in his jacket that hadn't been ruined from being soaked in his own blood, and he figured there was a good chance Sarah wouldn't let him have one even if there was. But he supposed it wouldn't hurt to try. He called, "Miss Hodge? Sarah?"

She appeared in the open doorway a moment later. "What can I get you, Mr. Long?"

"Call me Custis," he said with a smile. "And I hate to bother you, but I was wondering if you might be able to find a cheroot in my jacket."

She frowned. "Dr. Barkley didn't say anything about letting you smoke."

Longarm had been afraid she would say that. He tried not to sigh. "I reckon I'll wait and ask him when he gets back with the sheriff. Wouldn't want you to do anything to get you in trouble."

Her face flushed, and he wondered if she was thinking about what she had done to him earlier. He kept his own features carefully expressionless until the moment passed. Sarah said, "It shouldn't be much longer now. Sheriff Hampton must not have been in his office when the doctor got there, and he had to go look for him."

"More than likely," Longarm agreed.

"But I know that Sheriff Hampton must be somewhere around town. He wouldn't miss the wedding for any reason. He's Brent's best man."

Once again Longarm had to struggle to keep surprise from showing on his face. "Best man, eh?" he said. "They must be pretty good pards."

"They've been friends for a long time, even though the sheriff's a little older. I'm pretty sure they knew each other even before Brent came here and bought the Circle C."

Longarm made himself nod as if he were only mildly

interested in what she was telling him. Inside, though, his hopes were plummeting.

If Culhane and the sheriff were such good friends, as Sarah said they were, then chances were that Hampton knew exactly what Culhane had been up to. That meant the sheriff was crooked, too. Longarm could imagine a set-up in which Culhane and Hampton had once ridden the owlhoot trail together. Then Hampton had gone straight and become a lawman. But Culhane's arrival in the area would have knocked that in a cocked hat. Hampton would have had to go along with Culhane's scheme or risk having his own outlaw past revealed.

Or maybe Hampton was every bit as much of a killer as Culhane was and had just pretended to go straight. It didn't really matter right now, Longarm realized. What was important was that he couldn't tell Hampton who he was and what had really happened out there on the desert. If he did, Hampton would either tip off Culhane—or try to kill Longarm himself.

There was a chance Hampton didn't know anything about Culhane's search for the stranger who had stumbled onto the secret of the *Llano Caliente* and killed several of his men. If Culhane hadn't been in Bell City for the past day or so, he wouldn't have had the chance to tell Hampton about it.

"That beau of yours has probably been spending a lot of time in town lately," Longarm said, making the words sound like an idle comment. "What with the wedding coming up and all."

"Oh, no. It's bad luck for the groom to see the bride during the last week before the wedding. Brent's been staying on his ranch all the time."

Longarm had heard variations on that superstition before. He was glad it was one Sarah seemed to believe in. He couldn't be sure that Culhane hadn't slipped into Bell City to tell Hampton that their scheme was in danger, but at least it increased the possibility that he hadn't.

Footsteps sounded, and Sarah turned toward the front of the house. "Oh, here they are now," she said.

A moment later, Doc Barkley appeared in the doorway, followed by a tall, beefy man with powerful shoulders and a florid face. The second man had a sheriff's star pinned to his brown vest.

"You're sitting up," Barkley said when he saw Longarm. "I'm not sure that's a good idea."

"That broth Miss Sarah fed me made me feel a whole heap better," Longarm said. That was true, as far as it went. Of course, the things she had told him about Brent Culhane and Sheriff Hampton had made him feel worse again after that.

The lawman stepped forward. "Clyde Hampton," he introduced himself. "I'm the sheriff in these parts. Doc tells me your name is Long?"

Longarm nodded. "That's right. Custis Long." He hoped Hampton hadn't heard of him, didn't know that he was a star packer, too. It was pure luck that he hadn't said anything to Sarah or Doc Barkley about being a deputy U.S. marshal. Now that he was aware of the connection between Hampton and Culhane, he knew it was vital that he keep the information to himself until he'd figured out what to do next.

"And somebody bushwhacked you out on the desert?" Hampton prodded.

Longarm would have preferred it if nobody in Bell City even knew that he'd come across the *Llano Caliente*, but it was too late to do anything about that now. He nodded and said, "That's right, Sheriff. I'm afraid I can't help you much when it comes to finding whoever done it, though. You see, I never got a good look at the scoundrel."

Hampton frowned. "There aren't many places to hide in a desert. How was somebody able to shoot you without you seeing him?"

"There're more places than you might think," Longarm said. "The fella ventilated me from the top of one of those dunes. I heard the shot at the same time the bullet hit me and knocked me out of the saddle. My horse took off and never looked back. I reckon the gent who did the shooting figured he'd killed me, because he didn't come and check. After a while I was able to get up and start walking."

"And you wound up here," Hampton said with a grunt. "When did this happen?"

"Late yesterday afternoon."

"What were you doing in the desert? Most folks go the long way around, rather than try to cross it."

Longarm fell back on the same story he had used at first with Elizabeth. "I didn't have time to take the long way. I work for a land and cattle syndicate, and they're anxious for my report on this area. I checked out Rampart Valley, then somebody over there told me there were some good ranches on this side of the desert. So I thought I'd better take a look."

Hampton grunted again. Longarm couldn't tell if the lawman believed his story or not. There was nothing about it to make Hampton overly suspicious . . . unless, of course, he already knew about Longarm's encounter with Culhane.

After a moment, Hampton said, "Probably just some drifting owlhoot who took a potshot at you, Long. Don't know why he didn't try to rob you, though. Maybe it was an Indian. We still get a proddy buck or two showing up every now and then, off the reservations up north."

"I couldn't tell you one way or the other, Sheriff. Like I said, I never saw the fella."

Hampton nodded. "I hate to tell you this, but the chances of me being able to find whoever shot you are mighty slim. Any tracks the bushwhacker left are long gone by now. All it takes is a few hours of the wind blowing over that sand to wipe out any sign."

"I figured as much," Longarm said. "I knew I needed to report what happened, anyway."

"That's right, you did. And I'll keep my eyes and ears open. If I hear any talk about somebody taking a potshot at a stranger on the desert, I'll look into it right away."

"I'm much obliged, Sheriff." Longarm knew good and well Hampton wouldn't make any effort to investigate the shooting. He put a look of gratitude on his face, though, making him seem like an innocent pilgrim grateful for the opportunity to dump his troubles on a lawman.

Any hope of being able to maintain that pose would vanish as soon as Hampton had a chance to talk to Culhane, which would be later this afternoon at the wedding. Until then, Longarm had bought himself some time.

Hampton said his good-byes and left the house. Dr. Barkley leaned over the bed to check on the dressings wrapped around Longarm's middle and nodded in satisfaction. "Looks like the bleeding is still stopped," he commented. "I'll go back to my office and fix up a place for you, Long. Then, I'll drive over here in my buggy to get you and take you back there."

Longarm nodded. "All right, Doc."

Barkley glanced over at Sarah and asked, "You don't mind looking after Mr. Long for a little while longer?"

"Of course not," she replied. "He hasn't been much bother."

"Well, we'll both be out of your hair soon enough, and you can get on with getting ready for the wedding. What time is Mrs. Hutchins supposed to be over to help you get dressed?"

"She said she'd be here at three."

"We'll be out of here long before that," Barkley said. He gave Longarm a nod and bustled out of the room. A moment later, Longarm heard the front door of the house open and shut.

Sarah hesitated in the doorway. "I don't want you to

feel like I'm being inhospitable, Mr. Long . . ."

"Nope, not a bit," Longarm assured her. "You've already done more for me than most folks would have."

She smiled at him and said as she had earlier, "Call me if you need anything."

When she was gone, Longarm leaned his head against the pillow again and let the wheels of his brain revolve, picking up speed gradually as he tried to figure a way out of this mess. The thing to do, he decided, was to let Barkley move him over to the doctor's office. Barkley would be going to the wedding, so Longarm would be left there alone. As soon as Barkley was gone, Longarm would have to get out of the office and find himself another hiding place. Hampton knew that was where he was being taken, and as soon as Culhane alerted Hampton to the danger of Longarm remaining alive, Hampton would come looking for him to kill him. Longarm had to be somewhere else by then.

He wasn't sure how well he could get around. He was still mighty weak, and the lightheadedness and chills he felt from time to time told him that his fever hadn't broken. Gone down a little, maybe, but it was still there.

He could move easier, though, now that his side was bandaged up. The tight dressing would keep the wound from breaking open so easily. Longarm thought his mind and eyes were clear enough so that he could shoot if he had to, also. He was far from being a hundred percent, but if he had to, he would fight like a cornered cougar.

That thought made Longarm glance toward his gun. He had been so famished when Sarah brought in that broth that he'd forgotten to ask her to move the Colt within reach. Then Barkley and Hampton had showed up. Longarm really wanted the gun where he could get to it. He shifted around in the bed and leaned toward the table. He thought he could reach the butt of the revolver if he really stretched out.

Instead, his head suddenly spun crazily, and he felt his balance deserting him. He made a grab at the sheet, but his fingers slipped. With a muffled curse, he fell halfway off the bed.

Sarah must have heard the slight commotion. With a rapid patter of footsteps, she came down the hall from the kitchen and hurried into the bedroom. "Mr. Long!" she exclaimed. "What in the world are you doing?"

Awkwardly, Longarm looked up at her. "Custis," he reminded her. "You're supposed to call me Custis."

"I think I should call you a foolish man for trying to get out of bed. Is that what you were trying to do? If you need the, ah, chamber pot, I'll be glad to get it for you."

"No, thanks," Longarm said. His partially upside down position was causing his head to pound and making him dizzier than ever. "Just help me back up into the bed."

She came to his side and bent down to grasp his arm. "Of course. I just hope you haven't reinjured yourself. The doctor won't like it if he comes back to find you bleeding again."

Longarm didn't like the idea of that, either. He pushed himself up while Sarah pulled, and between them they got him upright in the bed again. Sarah was leaning close to him, and he became aware that the soft, warm pressure on his upper arm came from her breast. Sarah had to know that, too, but she didn't move back. Instead she asked, "Are you all right? Can you tell if the wounds are bleeding again?"

"I don't think so," Longarm replied honestly. "They feel just the same to me."

Sarah straightened at last. "All right. I'm glad. Just don't try to get up again until the doctor gets back with his buggy."

Longarm nodded. "There's just one more thing . . ."

"What is it?"

He pointed to the Colt resting in its holster and the

135

attached shell belt. "Would you mind shoving that smoke pole over here a mite closer?"

Sarah frowned and didn't move toward the gun. "That's what you were after? Why? You don't need a gun right now, do you?"

"Probably not, but I'm used to having a six-shooter close at hand just in case. Besides, somebody took a shot at me yesterday. He might've followed me here."

"That's very unlikely," Sarah said, but Longarm thought he saw a flicker of worry in her eyes. "You're safe in Bell City. The sheriff doesn't allow any lawbreakers within miles of this town."

Longarm didn't really doubt that. Hampton wouldn't want anybody horning in on whatever arrangement he had with Culhane.

"I reckon that's true, but I'd still feel better if that gun was just a little closer," he said.

Sarah sighed. "All right, if you insist." She moved Colt, holster, and belt across the table toward the bed. "Is that where you want it?"

"Yes, ma'am, that'll do fine. Thank you."

"I don't want any gunplay in my house, though," she said sternly.

"Me, neither," Longarm agreed and meant it. He wanted to be somewhere else, some place he could fort up if he needed to, before he had to do any more shooting.

He heard the front door open, and Sarah did, too. She turned her head in that direction as footsteps sounded in the hall. "Dr. Barkley must be back—" she began.

She stopped as a man's voice called, "Miss Sarah? Are you here? The boss sent me to bring this to you, since he can't see you himself—" The voice stopped short as the man stepped into the open doorway. He wore range clothes and carried a small package wrapped in bright paper in his left hand. His eyes widened in surprise as he

136

saw Sarah standing there next to the bed where Longarm was sitting.

Longarm and the newcomer recognized each other at the same instant. The last time they had seen each other was out on the *Llano Caliente*, when Longarm had been a prisoner of the rustlers.

"Damn!" the man exclaimed. "It's him!"

His right hand flashed toward the gun on his hip.

Chapter 13

Longarm's instincts took over. He twisted in the bed, his right hand reaching for the butt of his Colt while the left shot out to give Sarah a hard shove on her hip. The push sent her stumbling toward the wall, out of the line of fire. She cried out in surprise.

Under normal circumstances, Longarm wouldn't have had any trouble beating Culhane's man to the draw. But these circumstances were anything but normal. He was injured, feverish, and in an awkward position on the bed. In addition, when he grabbed the Colt, the holster came with it instead of the gun sliding free smoothly like it usually did. By that time, the rustler had his revolver out, and the barrel was coming up to line itself on Longarm. The big lawman saw that he was going to a shade too late . . .

Instead of a gun blast, there was a loud thud. The outlaw's gun sagged as he stumbled forward a step and went to one knee. Longarm saw Doc Barkley behind the man, medical bag upraised to strike another blow. The rustler was more startled than he was hurt, and Longarm knew it would be only a matter of seconds before he recovered his wits.

There was a flash of brown and tan as Dobie launched himself at the rustler. The little dog's teeth fastened on the man's gun wrist. The outlaw yelled and tried to shake Dobie loose. Barkley hit him again with the bag.

Longarm shook the Colt out of the holster, rolled off the bed, landed unsteadily on his feet, and reversed the gun in his hand. Putting one hand on the footboard for balance, he lunged at the outlaw. The Colt swept up and then down, and the butt of the gun crashed against the outlaw's skull. The man's eyes rolled up in their sockets. He toppled forward onto his face, out cold.

Longarm's pulse hammered wildly. That had been close, damned close. And he wasn't out of the woods yet, not by a long shot. Sarah and Barkley were both staring at him.

"What have you done to Hughey?" Sarah demanded. Her face was white with anger as she stepped over to confront Longarm.

"You saw him," Longarm said. "He went for his gun first."

"I saw that from just outside the room," Doc Barkley said. "I didn't want somebody shooting you right after I'd patched you up, Long, so I hit him. But that doesn't explain what the devil's going on here. You'd better talk and talk fast, or I'm going to get the sheriff."

Longarm's strength was fading. He turned the Colt around again, so that he was gripping the butt once more, and sank down on the edge of the bed. He pointed with his other hand at the unconscious outlaw and said, "This is one of Culhane's men." It wasn't a question.

Sarah answered anyway. "Of course he is. His name is Hughey. Why did you hit him like that?"

"To keep him from killing me." Longarm took a deep breath. His original plan was shot to hell now. He would have to tell Sarah and Barkley the truth and hope he could

139

make them believe it. "He recognized me. You saw that for yourself."

"He certainly seemed to," Barkley agreed.

"That's because he was with the bunch in the desert that tried to kill me."

Barkley regarded Longarm with narrowed eyes. "I knew you were lying to the sheriff about that part of the story. That wound in your side didn't happen as recently as when you said. I couldn't figure out, though, why you weren't telling the truth."

"Because it's Culhane who wants me dead, and he and Hampton are partners."

Sarah gasped. "That's a lie!" she said. "Brent and his men wouldn't try to hurt you." Her eyes widened as another thought occurred to her. "Unless you're some sort of outlaw!"

"You've got that backwards, Miss Sarah," Longarm told her. "I'm a deputy United States marshal. And Culhane and his men are the rustlers who've been stopping cattle trains over in Rampart Valley and stealing the herds."

Barkley rubbed his jaw. "Rustlers, you say? I've heard about that."

Sarah turned a furious gaze toward him. "Doctor! Surely you don't believe what this man is saying?"

"Right now, I'm not sure what to believe," Barkley said. "Keep talking, Long . . . if that's really your name."

Longarm nodded and said, "It is. You can wire Chief Marshal Vail in Denver and ask him."

"I could if there was a telegraph office in Bell City," Barkley said. "Closest one is in Rossville."

There went one of Longarm's ideas. He had hoped to convince Barkley of the truth and get the doctor to wire Billy Vail for some help.

The man on the floor groaned and stirred a little. Longarm looked down at him and said to the doctor, "You'd

140

better tie up this hombre while you've got the chance, or we'll have some real trouble on our hands."

"I think we have plenty of real trouble already," Barkley said in dry tones. But then he looked at Sarah and asked, "Have you got some cord or rope around here?"

"Doc, have you lost your mind? We can't trust anything this man says."

"Just get the rope," Barkley snapped. "That way we can figure this out without any gunplay."

"Hold on," Longarm said. "Miss Sarah, you'd best stay right here. Doc, use some bandages from your bag. That'll do to tie him up."

"Now you don't trust me," Sarah accused. "You think I'd go for the sheriff."

Longarm looked at her and said, "That's exactly what I think, ma'am. No offense, but I need you and Doc right here where I can keep an eye on the two of you."

Sarah looked at Barkley. "That ought to be enough right there to tell you that Mr. Long can't be trusted."

"He's just being cautious." Barkley shook his bag gently. Longarm heard rattling inside. Barkley sighed and said, "I probably broke every bottle and phial in there when I walloped Hughey with it. I didn't really think about what I was doing when I came in behind him and saw him going for his gun. I just hope I did the right thing."

"You did, Doc," Longarm told him. "You'll see when I've told you all of it."

While Sarah stood by with her arms crossed over her bosom and a disapproving frown on her face, Barkley took several strips of bandage and tied Hughey's hands securely behind his back. The doctor suggested that the outlaw be gagged, too. Barkley used a wad of cotton for that, tying it in place with another dressing.

When he was finished with that task, Barkley straightened and said, "All right, Long. Convince me that I'm not crazy for believing you a little bit."

"You might ought to sit down, Doc. This'll take a while. You, too, Miss Sarah."

She sniffed. "I'm fine where I am, thank you."

"All right, if you say so." As Barkley took one of the straight-backed chairs in the room, Longarm launched into a recitation of the events that had brought him to Bell City, starting with his investigation in Castleton. The only thing he left out was any mention of what he and Elizabeth Townsend had done together in the hayloft of her livery barn and out there on the desert. Barkley, being a male, might have guessed at it, but Longarm wasn't going to provide any details.

When he came to the part about Culhane, Sarah interrupted to say flatly, "I don't believe you. Brent is not an outlaw and a rustler."

"You may not want to believe it, ma'am, but those are the facts," Longarm said. "He and his men tried more than once to kill me."

"You can't prove that. You can't even prove that you're a federal marshal."

"Not right now, I can't. But as soon as I can get in touch with the chief marshal in Denver, he'll vouch for me."

"I don't think Mr. Long would be foolish enough to make a claim so easily verified unless it was true, Sarah," Barkley put in.

"Unless he's just trying to stall us," she shot back. "You told him yourself that there's no telegraph office here, Doc. He knows it would take time to check out his story."

Barkley looked at Longarm, and Longarm shrugged. "What can I tell you, Doc? She's right about that. But what I've told you about Culhane and those stolen cows and those wells he blasted out of the desert, all that's the gospel."

Down on the floor, Hughey made angry noises. He was awake now, and Longarm supposed he was trying to deny the accusations Longarm was making. The gag in his mouth prevented that, though.

Barkley studied Longarm. "And Sheriff Hampton's part of this scheme, you say?"

"I don't have any evidence of that," Longarm admitted. "But Sarah said Hampton and Culhane know each other from way back. It makes sense that if Culhane was going to set up a rustling ring, he'd bring an old pard in on it. Especially if the hombre was now a lawman who could shield Culhane if any outside investigators came nosing around —like me."

Slowly, Barkley nodded. "You could be right. About all of it."

"Doc!" Sarah exclaimed.

Barkley looked at her and said, "Listen to me, Sarah. I never fully trusted Brent Culhane. Oh, I was willing to put aside my reservations about him, because I figured if you had agreed to marry him, he must be all right. I thought you saw qualities in him that I never did. But I was still worried about this marriage. I felt like I owed it to your father to see that you were happy and taken care of, since he and I were friends for so many years. I planned to keep a close eye on young Culhane—" He broke off with a shake of his head. "You won't believe it until you see it with your own eyes, will you?"

"No, I won't," Sarah said. "And that means I'll never believe it, because it's not true."

Longarm pointed down at Hughey. "Then how come this fella reached for his gun as soon as he saw me?"

Sarah frowned. For a long moment, she didn't say anything, then she ventured, "Maybe you're the outlaw. Maybe Hughey and some of the other Circle C hands caught you stealing cattle. They shot at you, and you were wounded. That would explain everything just as well as that pipe dream of yours did."

Longarm shrugged. "Maybe."

"There's no maybe about it. You know I'm right. *You're* the rustler, and I ought to go fetch Sheriff Hampton right now to arrest you."

Longarm hefted the Colt in his hand and said, "That wouldn't be a good idea."

"You wouldn't shoot me," Sarah said as she gave him a haughty stare. "You wouldn't dare."

Longarm smiled humorlessly and said, "I reckon you're right. I wouldn't shoot you. But if you go tell Hampton what I've just told you and the doc, you'll be signing my death warrant, Miss Sarah."

Barkley said, "If you're right about Hampton, he's going to be gunning for you as soon as he talks to Culhane this afternoon, anyway."

"Yep," Longarm agreed. "That's why I've got to get out of here and find some other place to lay low for a while. It won't be safe here or at your office, Doc."

"No, those are the first places Hampton and Culhane will look." Barkley turned a level, intense gaze on the young woman. "Sarah, I believe what Long has told us. Will you give him the benefit of the doubt and help him?"

"When he wants to hurt the man I'm going to marry?" She shook her head. "No. I can't."

"Then will you at least be quiet about this, so that I can have a chance to get Marshal Long out of town?"

Sarah hesitated, and for a moment Longarm didn't know what her answer was going to be. Then, finally, she said, "I suppose I could do that."

"Good," Longarm said. "I'm much obliged, ma'am. You've helped a lot so far, and you still are."

"Don't remind me," she snapped. "I'm beginning to wish I'd left you out there by the shed."

Longarm didn't doubt that for a second.

He turned back to Barkley and pointed at the trussed-up gunman again. "We've got to do something about this gent."

"I won't be a party to cold-blooded murder."

"Never figured you would, Doc. I was thinking more along the lines of stashing him out back in the shed. You can tie his feet so he can't get loose."

"Won't Culhane wonder why he never came back?"

"He can wonder," Longarm said. "That's still better than turning Hughey loose to spill our plans."

Barkley grunted in agreement with that argument.

Meanwhile, Sarah picked up the package that Hughey had carried into the room when he arrived. He had dropped it during the brief flurry of action, and it had been forgotten until now. Sarah said, "This must be some sort of present," and began tearing open the wrapping paper.

She pulled the paper back and revealed a small box. When she opened it, she caught her breath and said, "Oh! It's lovely."

She lifted out a large, beautiful flower. A desert rose, Longarm thought. Almost as pretty as Sarah herself.

"There's a note with it," she said. Her voice threatened to break. "He . . . he wants me to wear it pinned to my wedding gown." She turned sharply to face Longarm. "How am I supposed to believe that such a sweet man is the killer and cattle thief you make him out to be?"

"I don't know what to tell you, Miss Sarah. Most folks have good and bad both mixed up inside them. Must be you bring out whatever good Culhane has left in him."

Sarah looked down at the blossom in her hand and said in a hollow voice, "I wish you had never crossed the *Llano Caliente*, Mr. Long."

Longarm thought about Elizabeth Townsend and how she had died, and he said, "I reckon in a way I agree with you, Miss Sarah."

• • •

Doc Barkley tied Hughey's feet together as securely as the outlaw's wrists were tied. Hughey tried to kick and fight at first, until Longarm reached down and put the barrel of the Colt against his temple. After that, his struggles subsided, and Barkley finished trussing him up.

Then it was up to Barkley to drag Hughey outside and hide him in the shed. The medico was puffing and blowing when he came back to the house, and sweat beaded on his brightly flushed face. "I'm not accustomed to hauling around so much dead weight," he complained.

"Well, at least he wasn't really dead," Longarm pointed out.

"Yes, there's that to be said." Barkley took out a handkerchief and mopped his face. As he put it away, he looked at Longarm and went on, "Now, what are we going to do with you?"

"I'm open to suggestions, Doc. Is there any place in town I can hide where Culhane and Hampton can't find me?"

With a frown, Barkley considered the question. "Bell City isn't that big a place," he said. "If Culhane's crew gets in on the hunt, they could search every house and business in just a few hours. We could try shifting you around from place to place, but that would be pretty risky."

"Too risky," Longarm said with a shake of his head. "You said something earlier about getting me out of town. I reckon that'd be the best idea. Bring your buggy around the back. I'll climb in and lay down behind the seat, and you can cover me up with an old blanket or something."

Barkley nodded. "That sounds like it might work. Jouncing around in the back of a buggy isn't going to be very comfortable for you, though—and it's not going to do that bullet wound much good, either."

"Can't be helped."

"No, I suppose not. It would be much more unhealthful to wait here for Culhane to show up."

Sarah was sitting in a rocking chair in the corner, arms crossed, forehead creased in a frown. She had kept silent while Hughey was taken out and while Longarm and Barkley made their plans, but now she said, "He's got you completely convinced now, doesn't he, Doctor? You really believe Brent is the villain he makes him out to be."

"I still don't know what I believe," Barkley said testily, "but I'm going to err on the side of saving a man's life. If Long is lying, I'll do what I can to set things straight later. In the meantime, I won't stand by and take a chance on watching him be killed."

Sarah sighed, looked away, and didn't say anything else. Longarm felt a pang of regret at the young woman's reaction. He would have liked to convince her that he was telling the truth, too. He owed her a debt of gratitude, and he hated to think of how Culhane had deceived her. But there was nothing else he could say, nothing more he could do, to open her eyes. He hoped that when Sarah finally did discover the truth about the man she had planned to marry, it wouldn't hurt her too much.

"I'll bring the buggy around," Barkley told Longarm.

"All right, Doc. I'll get my pants and boots on."

Barkley went out. Longarm stood up, slipped the gun into its holster, and set them on the table. He reached for his denim trousers, which were draped over a nearby chair. As he did so, a wave of dizziness hit him. He had to grip the back of the chair to steady himself.

"Oh, for goodness sake," Sarah said as she stood up. "Let me help you."

Longarm looked at her. "Thought you had me figured for a desperado."

"Maybe I do, but I still don't want you falling down and opening up that wound again. Then you'd bleed all

147

over my floor. You've bled enough in my house today, Mr. Long."

Longarm smiled. "Don't reckon I can argue with that sentiment."

She picked up his trousers and knelt beside him. He lifted one foot, then the other, and let her work the legs of the garment onto them. Longarm became aware of how close her head was to his groin. Her shiny blond hair bobbed there just a few inches away from his manhood. That thought made the shaft start to swell and thicken.

If she noticed the lump in his long underwear as she pulled up the trousers, she gave no sign of it. Longarm felt less dizzy now, so he said, "Much obliged," and did all the buttoning and buckling himself. He didn't want Sarah's fingers prodding around at his crotch. Even though he was wounded, certain other parts of his anatomy still had a mind of their own, as usual.

"Sit down and I'll help you with your boots," Sarah said. Longarm complied, easing down on the edge of the bed. Again she knelt before him. She picked up the black stovepipes and worked them onto his feet and calves. Longarm stood up, stomped each foot to settle it in the boot, and reached for his gunbelt.

Sarah stayed where she was as he buckled on the belt. Looking up at him, she said, "Please, Mr. Long . . . don't kill Brent."

Longarm's jaw tightened. He didn't like this a bit. Kneeling and begging like that was beneath Sarah's dignity. He reached down, got hold of her under her arms, and lifted her to her feet. She didn't fight him, didn't try to pull away. He rested his hands on her shoulders and said, "Chances are you saved my life, ma'am, and I owe you for that. But I've got a job to do, and that means bringing Culhane to justice. I've never drawn on a man without giving him a chance to surrender, and I don't plan

148

to start now. I just can't make you no promises I may not be able to keep."

She looked away from him. "Of course. I don't know what I was thinking."

Longarm bit back a curse. Sometimes packing a badge—and all the responsibility that went with it—was a worrisome burden.

He let go of Sarah as he heard Barkley come into the house. She turned away and went back to the rocking chair. The doctor was rubbing his hands together as he came into the room. He nodded to Longarm and said, "I guess we're ready to go."

"All right, Doc."

"Wait a minute," Sarah said. "I still have some of my father's old shirts. I'll get one of them for you, Mr. Long. It'll be a little small, but better than nothing."

Longarm nodded. "I'm much obliged, Miss Sarah. I've been saying that to you a whole heap today, but it's true."

She hurried out of the room and came back a moment later with a brown plaid shirt. Longarm slipped it on, buttoned it, and rolled up the too-short sleeves a couple of turns. The shirt would make him less noticeable if anyone happened to see him. The white bandages swathing his torso really would have stood out if they'd been visible.

He never had gotten that cheroot, and he sure could have used a drink of Maryland rye, but those simple pleasures would have to wait. Right now his very survival was at stake. He followed Doc Barkley out of the bedroom, pausing at the door to look back a final time at Sarah. She stood by the window, her back stiff and straight, looking outside. Longarm didn't speak to her, just followed Barkley to the back door and out of the house.

The doctor's buggy was parked next to the shed, not far from where Sarah had found Longarm early that morning. A sturdy-looking gray horse was hitched to the vehicle. Longarm wasn't sure how visible the back yard was from the neighboring houses, so Barkley went first. After looking in all directions, he nodded to Longarm and said, "No one seems to be around. Come on."

Longarm stepped out of the house and walked toward the shed. He couldn't hurry too much, because each step made his wounded side ache. At least the sharp pains had subsided since the bullet holes had been cleaned and bandaged.

He reached the buggy and peered behind the seat. The space back there wasn't as big as he would have liked for it to be, but there was nothing to be done about that. He would have to crowd into it as best he could. Barkley took hold of the lawman's arm to help him as Longarm crawled into the buggy and lay down behind the seat. The black canvas cover arched up over him like a cathedral roof.

Barkley took a blanket off the seat and spread it over Longarm, who lay on his left side with his knees pulled up. The doctor tucked in the corners of the blanket around him.

"It'll be a mite hot in there, I expect," Barkley said quietly.

"Better hot than shot at," Longarm replied, his voice muffled by the blanket. He was already sweating. It seemed his fever had broken, and he was glad of that. It was going to be warm enough under here without burning up from the inside out.

He felt the springs of the buggy give as Barkley stepped up into the vehicle and settled himself on the seat. A moment later, Barkley called out to the horse, and the buggy jolted into motion. The movement was a little painful, but not too bad.

"Nobody's going to pay too much attention to me," Barkley said as he drove. "I travel all over this part of the country tending to folks who are sick or hurt. Nobody minds a doctor's comings and goings."

Longarm hoped Barkley was right. It was possible, though, that Culhane would have some of his men watching the town. They might report to the boss outlaw that Barkley had left Bell City.

Don't get ahead of yourself and start borrowing trouble, old son, he told himself. Just eat the apple one bite at a time—and watch out for worms.

The buggy turned a corner. Longarm hadn't gotten a look at the rest of Bell City, only the backyard of Sarah's place and the inside of her house, so he didn't know anything about where they were or what route they needed to take out of town. He would have to rely completely on Barkley for that. After a few moments, the buggy turned again.

Then it slowed abruptly, and Barkley called out to the horse. Under his breath, he added, "Damn it!"

"What's wrong?" Longarm asked, as quietly as possible, hoping that Barkley would have the sense not to turn around when he answered. It would look mighty funny if the doctor started talking directly to a blanket in the back of the buggy.

"It's Clyde Hampton," Barkley said, so faint that Longarm could barely hear him. "He waved for me to stop. Here he comes, Long."

And all Longarm could do was lie there in the dark under the blanket, sweat dripping off his face, his fingers wrapped tightly around the butt of the gun in his hand.

Chapter 14

"Hey, Doc, where are you going?" Sheriff Hampton asked in a booming voice. Longarm heard the question plainly from where he lay underneath the blanket.

"Got to see a patient out of town," Barkley answered.

"Oh? Who might that be?"

Barkley hesitated, then said, "Eb Mullins down at the Slash M. He sent one of his punchers in to tell me that Eb's lumbago is acting up again something terrible."

"Sorry to hear that. 'S funny, though. I haven't seen any of Eb's riders in town today."

"He must've started back to the ranch in a hurry," Barkley said. "You know how Mullins is about his men not wasting any of the time he's paying them for."

Hampton laughed. "Eb's a tight man with a dollar, that's for sure. Tell the old coot I hope he gets better."

"I'll do that, Sheriff." Though Longarm couldn't see it, he could imagine Barkley lifting the reins and getting ready to start the horse moving again.

"Say, Doc," Hampton went on, a note of worry in his voice now, "you're going to be back in time for the big wedding this afternoon, aren't you?"

"Well, I don't rightly know. It's a quite a long way down to the Mullins's spread."

"Sarah would sure be disappointed if you couldn't be there. You and her father were friends for a long time, weren't you?"

"Over ten years," Barkley said.

"I hope you make it back, then."

"I'll try, but caring for the sick has to come first, before any personal wishes. The Hippocratic oath, you know."

"Sure. You get that stranger moved over to your office?"

Longarm had wondered when Hampton would get around to asking about that.

"Yes, I took him over there a little while ago."

"Won't he need somebody to look after him while you're gone?"

Longarm's jaw tightened. If Hampton offered to look in on him between now and the wedding, it would complicate matters.

"No, he'll be fine until I get back. I've got him settled in that room I use for patients I have to keep there overnight. In fact, I gave him something to make him sleep. Rest is what he needs more than anything else."

"Yeah, I reckon," Hampton said. "Still, I was hoping to ask him a few more questions about that bushwhacking."

"It'll have to be later," Barkley said, his voice stern and weighted with all his medical authority.

"Sure, Doc. Well, I better not keep you, or you definitely won't get back in time for the wedding."

"So long, Clyde," Barkley said, and this time he whipped the buggy horse into motion so quickly that the sheriff didn't have the chance to detain him again.

After a few minutes of brisk trotting that made Longarm grit his teeth against the ache in his side, Barkley slowed the buggy and said, "That was too damned close."

"Where are we?" Longarm asked.

"We're out of town now."

Longarm pulled the blanket back from his face so that he could get some fresh air. He dragged in a couple of deep lungfuls, then said, "Hampton didn't seem to have any idea I was back here."

"No, I don't believe he did," Barkley agreed. "Let me get around this next curve in the road, and we'll be completely out of sight of the town."

A minute later, the doctor brought the buggy to a stop. Longarm threw the blanket back and sat up. He used the sleeve of his shirt to wipe sweat off his face, then looked around at the unfamiliar surroundings. The road had grassy, rolling plains to the left and some wooded hills rising to the right.

"We're south of Bell City?" he asked.

"Yes, this road runs all the way to Rossville."

"When the railroad builds that spur line up from there, it'll likely follow this route pretty close."

Barkley frowned at him. "You know about the spur line?"

"I've heard talk about it. When it gets to Bell City, Culhane will be able to dispose of all those beeves he's been rustling over in Rampart Valley. If he's smart, he'll ship them a few at a time, running them in with his own stock. It'll take a while, but he'll be a rich man by the time he's through. And he can keep it up as long as nobody knows about those wells out in the desert."

"What about the brands on the stolen cattle?"

"Brands can be reworked. If a fella's good enough with a running iron, there's no way to tell a brand has been changed short of killing and skinning the cow, so you can check the underside of the hide. With the stolen ones mixed in with Culhane's own stock, nobody will ever think to do that. Nobody will even suspect him of rustling."

154

Barkley grunted. "It sounds like you've thought out the whole thing."

"I've had some time to think the past couple of days," Longarm said with a grin. "When I wasn't being shot at or dragged around the desert or passing out, that is."

"Have you thought about what's going to happen to Sarah when it's revealed that her husband is a rustler and a killer?"

Longarm looked sharply at the doctor. "I was sort of hoping we could find a place for me to stay while you went back and talked Sarah out of marrying Culhane this afternoon. If she'd just postpone the wedding for a while, we can get a posse of marshals in here and clean up Culhane's rustling ring. Then Sarah can see for herself what sort of man he is."

"She'll never agree to that," Barkley said with a regretful shake of his head. "Her pride won't let her back out of marrying Culhane."

Longarm sighed. "It'll be bad for her later on, I reckon, when the truth comes out, but she'll have to be strong enough to go on and get over it. She won't be the first gal who's been taken in by a gent with a smooth line of gab."

"No, I suppose not." Barkley reached down to the floorboard and picked up his medical bag. As he opened it and began rummaging around inside it, he went on, "It would be better, though, if she never had to find out what Culhane's been up to."

Longarm frowned and said, "I don't hardly see how we could manage that."

Barkley turned around on the seat and thrust a small pistol over the back of it. The gun was pointed right at Longarm's head. "I do," Barkley said.

Longarm's eyes widened in surprise, but other than that, he didn't move. After a long, tense moment, he said, "Well, son of a bitch."

"Your arrival in Bell City has certainly complicated everything, Marshal Long."

"Oh, *now* you believe I'm a lawman."

"I believed you right away," Barkley said. "I told Culhane to leave the express cars alone on those trains, but he's always been the wild sort, unable to listen to reason, and those men who ride for him are even worse. I told him that if he bothered the mail, he'd bring some federal law down on us. Maybe the next time, he'll have sense enough to listen to me."

Still a little light-headed from his injury, Longarm felt his brain really starting to whirl now, his thoughts twisting and turning like a cyclone as he tried to make sense of what was happening. "I reckon you must be the one who figured out the whole thing," he said to Barkley.

"Most of it," the doctor said. "Step out of the buggy, Long. I'm getting tired of sitting turned around like this."

Slowly, Longarm climbed out of the vehicle. The barrel of Barkley's gun followed him the whole time, never wavering. The doctor—or boss rustler, Longarm thought—was an icy-nerved bastard.

Barkley stepped down from the buggy, too, and kept the gun pointed at Longarm as he did so. There was a smirk on his face as he said, "No doubt you're confused."

"Not too much. I ain't sure why you walloped ol' Hughey on the head, though, instead of letting him plug me."

"Sarah, of course. I couldn't let bullets start flying around that room and take a chance that she'd be hit. Even if she wasn't hurt, having you killed right there in front of her could have upset things even worse than they already were. If Hughey had the sense God gave a goat, he would have handed over that present Culhane sent and got out of there."

"And if he had, Sarah wouldn't have wondered why he ignored the gunshot man in her bed?"

Barkley shrugged. "Like I said, your mere presence was already causing considerable problems, Long. Luckily, once you'd told your story, Sarah herself came up with reasons not to believe it."

"You tried to convince her I was telling the truth," Longarm pointed out.

"Not really. I just played devil's advocate. I've known that girl for years. I knew how she'd react. Everything you said and everything I said just made her more stubbornly convinced that Brent Culhane really is the knight in shining armor that she believes him to be."

Longarm grimaced. Barkley was smooth, all right. The doctor had fooled Longarm, just as he had fooled Sarah. And he had gotten Hughey gagged quickly enough so that the gunman couldn't reveal the connection between him and Culhane.

"So it was all an act you put on. You just wanted to get me out of Sarah's house and out of town before I could talk her into believing what I was saying about Culhane."

"That's right. And when I walk back into town in a little while, I'll tell her that you admitted you were lying and that you stole my buggy to make your escape. You see, Long, in Sarah's eyes, you'll always be the rustler, not her darling husband."

"All this for Sarah's sake," Longarm murmured. "Why, Barkley? Just because you and her pa were friends?"

"Hardly. Don't you know that Sarah is a wealthy young woman?"

"How would I know that?" Longarm asked. "I never met her before this morning."

"Milt Hodge owned most of Bell City. More importantly, he owned a lot of the land between here and Rossville . . . land that the railroad will use as right-of-way for that spur line."

The light dawned for Longarm. "And now Sarah owns that land."

Barkley nodded. "Exactly. But after five o'clock this afternoon, it'll belong to her new husband . . . and his silent partner."

"You," Longarm said.

Barkley just smiled.

"It's a hell of a note," Longarm said bitterly, "when one of the town's leading citizens—a doctor, for God's sake—turns out to be the biggest crook of all."

"Yes, it is, isn't it?" Barkley said, not sounding the least bit contrite. "A doctor in a little cowtown is never going to get rich. But a partner in a spur line and a successful ranching operation, that's a different story. He's a man who's going to get rich."

"How many partners you got? What's Sheriff Hampton think about all this?"

"Hampton doesn't know a damned thing about it."

"I had the notion that him and Culhane used to ride together."

"They did," Barkley said, "but the fool really did go straight. He thinks Culhane did, too. No, we don't have to worry about Hampton." He motioned with the pistol. "And pretty soon we won't have to worry about you, either, Long. There's been enough palavering. Get over there in those trees."

Longarm didn't move. "Figure to gun me down, do you?"

"Of course. There's a ravine over there that'll make a good place to dispose of your body. Then I'll spin that little yarn I mentioned for Sarah, and everything can go back to normal around here."

Longarm shook his head. "I ain't moving, Doc. If you want to kill me, you'll have to do it right here and then drag me over to that ravine."

Barkley's lips drew back from his teeth. "Don't think

158

I won't if I have to. I hauled Hughey out to the shed, didn't I?"

"You didn't look too good when you got back, though," Longarm pointed out. "Fact is, the way you were huffing and blowing and turning red in the face, I'd say maybe that ticker of yours ain't in such good shape, Doc. You have to drag a big galoot like me around, you might just up and have a spell that'd kill you. You're a sawbones; you ought to know that." He grinned. "But what's that old saying about a doc who treats himself having a fool for a patient?"

Barkley flushed angrily. "Damn it, I'm tired of this. Get in the trees, Long, or by God, I *will* shoot you here and now!"

Longarm didn't doubt it, but while he had been talking, he was also edging his hand closer and closer to the corner of the blanket that had concealed him on the trip out of Bell City. It was dangling off the floorboard of the buggy and was almost within reach.

"Sarah's going to figure out sooner or later what sort of polecats you and Culhane are," he said, still stalling. "Then what'll you do?"

"It won't matter by then," Barkley snapped. "Everything will have been transferred into Culhane's name. And even if it's not . . . as her husband, he'll inherit everything should something happen to her." He lifted the gun a little more. "Now, are you going to——"

Longarm gasped and raised his right hand to his wounded side as if in pain. Barkley's eyes flicked toward the motion, and in that same instant, Longarm's left hand shot out and snagged the blanket. He jerked it out of the buggy and flung it at Barkley, who was so startled that he let out a yell. The gun in his hand cracked, sending a bullet tugging through the fabric of the blanket. The shot went wild, though, missing Longarm by several feet. Longarm was already moving in the other direction. His right hand reached across his body, moving at half of its normal speed as he palmed out the Colt. But in this case, half-speed was plenty. He triggered twice, firing through the blanket as it settled over Barkley's head.

Barkley staggered back, his face and upper body obscured by the blanket. The little pistol dropped out of his hand and thudded to the ground at his feet. He swayed one way, then the other, and then he pitched forward to land face down on the ground, his head still covered by the blanket. After a moment, a crimson pool began to edge out from under the fabric.

Longarm put his free hand on the buggy to brace himself. He hadn't been shamming when he reached for his side, not completely, though his intent had been to distract Barkley. The bullet wound did hurt, but not so much that he couldn't keep moving. He *had* to keep moving. Barkley was either dead or soon would be, but back in Bell City, the minutes were ticking by, bringing Sarah Hodge closer and closer to marrying Culhane. Longarm couldn't allow that to happen, not if he could stop it.

So this wasn't over. Not by a long shot.

Chapter 15

"My, but don't you look *lovely*, Sarah!" Mrs. Hutchins rubbed her plump hands together. "Land's sake, girl, I think you're just about the prettiest bride I ever did see!"

Sarah managed a weak smile as she sat at her dressing table. "Thank you."

"That Brent Culhane, he just doesn't know what a lucky man he is to be marrying a girl like you."

"I'm the lucky one," Sarah said.

She was able to form the words. Why didn't she believe them?

She looked at herself in the mirror as white-haired Mrs. Hutchins bustled around, adjusting the veil of fine white lace. Her blond hair was gathered into a thick braid at the back of her neck. She wore a high-necked white gown decorated with pearls and lace. The desert rose Brent Culhane had sent her was pinned to the bodice. The veil hung in front of her face, as it would when she entered the church later this afternoon, but it was so fine she had no trouble seeing through it to the troubled blue eyes underneath.

She had gone to bed the night before thinking that today would be happiest day of her life. But early this morning, when Dobie's barking had roused her from sleep, she was still groggy enough so that she hadn't given any thought to what day it was. She had just wanted to find out what had the little dog so upset. Then she had found the wounded stranger beside the shed, and all thoughts of marriage had fled from her brain as she coped with that unexpected development.

That had been just the beginning of a day filled with tension and violence and surprises. Sarah blushed fiercely as she thought about how she had fondled Custis Long and brought him to a release of his male passion. It was almost beyond belief to her that she had done such a thing, that she had acted so impulsively and rashly—and wantonly. If Mr. Long hadn't been a gentleman, he might have said something about that to Dr. Barkley, and then Sarah would have died of mortification.

But whatever else he might be—lawman, as he claimed, or rustler, as Sarah wanted to believe—he *was* a gentleman. She could not deny that. And if he had leveled his accusations of rustling and murder at almost anyone else in the world other than the man she was engaged to marry, Sarah might well have believed him. He had the look of a man who told the truth.

But she could not believe such things of Brent Culhane, not if she hoped to retain even a shred of her own pride. She would not believe that she had agreed to spend the rest of her life with such a man as Custis Long had described.

Mrs. Hutchins leaned in toward her, a frown of concern on the powdered and rouged face. "Dearie, you don't look happy at all. You should be overjoyed on a day like today."

"I know," Sarah said. "Maybe I'm just feeling a little nervous."

The older woman patted her on the shoulder. "Well, there's nothing wrong with that. Don't you worry about a thing, dear. Everything's going to be fine. In a little while, you'll be married, and you'll have the rest of a wonderful life in front of you."

"That's right," Sarah said, still looking at herself in the mirror. "A wonderful life."

Longarm lifted Doc Barkley's body and put it in the back of the buggy, then spread the blanket on top of the corpse to hide it. He was glad Barkley didn't weigh any more than he did. Given Longarm's wounded condition, it took enough of an effort to hoist the body into the vehicle as it was.

Then he climbed onto the seat and took out his gun to replace the two rounds he had fired. That gave him a chance to consider his options, as well. He could take up the reins and send the horse down the road toward Rossville. He wasn't sure how far it was, but he thought he could reach the junction by nightfall. Then he could send wires to Billy Vail and Sheriff Willard in Castleton and have help on the way immediately.

But if he did that, the wedding between Sarah Hodge and Brent Culhane would take place as planned. More than likely, Culhane would take Sarah out to the Circle C ranch house with him, and he would have her to use as a hostage when the posse showed up to arrest him and his men. There was a good chance that would lead to a pitched battle, Longarm thought—all of which meant that Sarah might wind up dead. And he didn't want that.

The other alternative wasn't much better. He fished his watch out of his pants pocket and checked the time. If he turned the buggy around and headed back to Bell City, he would get there well before the wedding. He couldn't fight Culhane and the rest of the gang by himself, though, especially not in the shape he was in.

But if he could get his hands on Sarah, he might be able to get her out of town and prevent the wedding that way. Then he could hotfoot it to Rossville and start yelling for help in cleaning up the rustling ring.

It was a risky plan, but the best he had available to him, Longarm decided. The trick would be in getting into town and back out again with Sarah without anyone seeing him.

He turned the buggy around and started back the way he and Barkley had come. He wasn't sure how far out of Bell City they were, so he took it slow. When he rounded a curve and could see the roofs of some of the buildings and the church steeple about a mile up the road, he hauled on the reins and steered the horse off to the left of the trail. When the buggy was hidden in a grove of trees, Longarm brought it to a stop. He would hoof it the rest of the way.

Before abandoning the buggy, though, he opened Barkley's medical bag and rooted around inside it, looking for anything that he might be able to use as a weapon. He found a small brown bottle with a cork in it, and when he pulled the cork and took a whiff of what was inside, he recognized the sweet, strong reek of ether. Longarm replaced the cork quickly before the stuff had a chance to make him any more light-headed. He stowed the bottle away in his pocket and tucked a couple of scalpels behind his belt. The bowie knife he had taken from the dead rustler Lewis was back at Sarah's somewhere. He had lost track of it during the confusion of the day.

Not knowing any details about the town would make it more difficult for him, he thought. He believed he would recognize Sarah's house if he could see the back of it, so he followed a course that would take him in a circle around the settlement. Each step was an effort. He was so weary he could have lain down and slept for a week. The strength he had gained earlier from the broth Sarah fed him was long since gone.

But he had this chore to do, and Longarm had never

164

been one to turn his back on a job just because it was hard. He kept moving, putting one foot in front of the other, lurching from tree to tree so that he could take advantage of their cover.

The sun moved across the afternoon sky while Longarm worked his way around Bell City. In his current condition, he had little sense of the passage of time. So it came as something of a surprise when he checked his watch again and found that the hour was now past three o'clock. He vaguely recalled some comment being made about one of the neighbor ladies coming over at three o'clock to help Sarah get dressed for the ceremony. By now, Sarah would be in her wedding gown.

Longarm was willing to bet that she was as pretty as a picture, too.

He forced that thought out of his head and tried to concentrate on the problem at hand, which was getting to Sarah's house and taking her out of there while he still had the chance. Would the neighbor stay with Sarah until it was time to go to the church? If that were the case, the woman's presence would be an extra problem. And what about Sarah herself? Would she fight him when he tried to take her? That seemed possible to Longarm, even likely. He could tell her about Doc Barkley revealing his own villainy and confirming Culhane's, but would Sarah believe that? Longarm didn't think so.

He paused, leaned against a tree, wiped the back of his hand across his mouth, sleeved sweat off his forehead. He wished he had a drink, even if it was water. His mouth was dry as could be.

After a moment, Longarm started walking again. He stumbled through brush, stopping from time to time to study the town through gaps in the foliage. The nearest house was no more than a hundred yards away. So far he hadn't seen any dwellings that he recognized. He kept his eyes open for the shed.

During the previous night, he had approached Bell City from the north. So it made sense that Sarah's house was somewhere on the north side of town. As he approached the section, he paid even closer attention. After several minutes, his efforts were rewarded. At least he hoped they were. He spotted a good-sized house, not overly fancy but solidly built, and behind it was a shed that looked familiar. Of course, more than one house in Bell City had a shed behind it, but Longarm was convinced this was the one he was looking for. He would have to cross about fifty yards of open space to reach the shed. After checking to make sure no one was in sight, he took a deep breath, pushed out of the brush, and broke into a shuffling run.

He was halfway to the shed when a little dog came out of it and started barking at him. Rather than being alarmed, Longarm was glad to see the animal. He recognized it as Dobie, Sarah's dog. As he stumbled up to lean against the shed, Dobie stopped barking and nosed around Longarm's leg. The dog must have recognized his scent and decided that Longarm was all right, because he got up on his hind legs and started prancing around, trying to get the lawman to pet him or play with him.

Longarm grinned down at the dog and said, "I'm glad to see you, too, Dobie." His use of the dog's name made Dobie dance around even more. "I hope your mistress is still inside."

For several minutes, Longarm rested against the wall. His pulse gradually slowed and he stopped breathing so hard. Feeling better, he edged to the corner and peered around it. The house was quiet.

His foot bumped something in the grass. He looked down and saw the bowie knife. He realized he must have dropped it there when he passed out the night before. Stooping, Longarm picked up the knife and added it to his collection of weapons.

There was no point in delaying. He had to get inside

the house. Summoning his strength, he catfooted toward the building, moving without his usual grace but still fairly silently.

When he reached the steps, he pressed his back against the wall and listened intently for a moment. He didn't hear any voices coming from inside the house, and he hoped that meant the neighbor lady was already gone. On the other hand, the silence might mean that Sarah had left for the church, in which case Longarm didn't know what he would do.

Only one way to find out, he told himself. He reached for the latch of the back door.

A rattle of hoofbeats from the front of the house made him stop in midmotion. What sounded like several riders came to a stop, and he heard low, male voices, though he couldn't make out what the men were saying. A moment later, a fist hammered on the front door of the house.

Then, a voice that Longarm recognized called out, "Sarah? Sarah, are you in there?"

Longarm's lips pulled back from his teeth in a grimace. *Culhane!* What was the rustler doing here, now of all times? He wasn't supposed to see Sarah until the wedding. He sure as hell wasn't supposed to see her in her wedding gown, and this close to the time of the ceremony, he had to know that she would be wearing the dress already.

Longarm leaned his head closer to the back door, trying to hear. He thought he heard the patter of quick footsteps inside the house, and sure enough, a second later Sarah said without opening the front door, "Brent, go away! You're not supposed to be here."

"Sarah, honey, I've got to talk to you," Culhane said.

"In a little while, we'll have the rest of our lives to talk. Please, Brent—"

Culhane interrupted her plea. "It's important, honey. Have you seen Hughey? I sent him into town earlier with something for you, and he never came back."

Longarm could tell that Sarah was hesitating before answering. As far as she knew, Longarm was being hidden out somewhere by Doc Barkley. Would she lie to her future husband in order to give Longarm more time to get away? Or, believing in Culhane, would she break down and confess to him everything that had happened?

After what seemed like a hell of a long time to Longarm, she said, "You mean the desert rose you sent me, Brent? It's lovely."

"Then Hughey *was* here?" Culhane asked.

"Of course."

"Where the devil did he go after that, then?"

"I . . . I'm afraid I don't know."

There it was, Longarm thought. She had lied for him, lied to the man she planned to marry in an hour or so. Would she have done that if she hadn't believed just a little, deep down, that there was a chance he had told her the truth about Culhane? He was filled with a new hope that maybe he could talk her into leaving with him willingly. But Culhane had to go away before that could happen.

"Brent," Sarah went on, "is . . . is something wrong?"

Longarm knew from her voice what she wanted to hear. She wanted Culhane to tell her that everything was fine, that there was nothing for her to worry about. She wanted to be reassured that the life she had planned out for them was going to come true. The events of this day had shaken her down to the core, had shaken her belief in everything she thought she knew. Now she wanted Culhane to put things right again.

Instead, Culhane said, "There's been some trouble. You haven't seen any strangers around town today, have you, Sarah?"

Longarm could almost see her catching her breath. She said, "I . . . haven't been away from the house. What's wrong, Brent? Who is this man you're looking for?"

168

"Forget it," Culhane said harshly. "It's not important right now. I'll find him later."

"You'll be at the church on time, won't you?"

"Of course I'll be there! I wouldn't let anything keep me away, honey."

Because he couldn't afford not to marry Sarah, Longarm thought. If anything happened to stop the wedding, the plot Culhane had hatched along with Doc Barkley might be ruined. They needed Sarah married to Culhane in order to control the land that would be used for the railroad spur line. Without the spur line, it would be harder to dispose of the rustled cattle. Everything dovetailed, and the linchpin holding it all together was Sarah.

"All right," she said. "I . . . I'll see you there."

Longarm waited to hear Culhane leave, but instead, after a few seconds, the rustler said, "Sarah, what's the matter? You sound like something's wrong."

"No, I . . . I'm fine," she replied, but even listening through the back door, Longarm could hear how unconvincing she sounded.

"Blast it, Sarah, is somebody in there with you? Somebody you're afraid of?"

Damn it, Longarm thought. Culhane was worried that he was in the house with Sarah! He could tell that much from Culhane's voice. The rustlers must have been combing the countryside all day looking for him, and it had occurred to Culhane that one of the last places he could expect to find his quarry was in the house of the woman he was about to marry! As Longarm stood there tensely, he thought about the twists of fate that had brought him first to Sarah's house, then away from it, and now back. Nobody could have anticipated such a thing beforehand, least of all Culhane.

"Of course I'm alone," Sarah said in reply to Culhane's question. "Mrs. Hutchins came over to help me dress, but

169

she's gone home to get ready for the wedding herself. Who else would be here?"

"You just sound so nervous, and there's a dangerous man on the loose in these parts. I reckon the boys and I ought to come in and have a look around."

"No!" Sarah cried, and Longarm thought she couldn't have sounded any more suspicious than she did. The funny thing was, she thought she was telling the truth. For all she knew, she was alone in the house. She had no idea he was crouched here by the back steps, eavesdropping. She went on, "You can't come in. You know that, Brent. It would be bad luck if you did."

Culhane grumbled something. Longarm couldn't make out the words, but he could sense the frustration Culhane must be feeling. He didn't want to go against Sarah's wishes, not when he was so close to getting everything he wanted, everything he had worked for. But he was desperate to find Longarm and shut him up before the lawman could tell anyone what he had discovered about the *Llano Caliente*.

"All right," Culhane said finally. "I'll see you in a little while at the church. So long, Sarah."

"Good-bye, Brent." The words came faintly from Sarah, so quietly Longarm could barely hear them.

He took a deep breath and waited for the sound of hoofbeats that would tell him Culhane and the rest of the gang were riding away. Before that could happen, Longarm heard something else: the scuff of boot leather on the ground.

And that sound came from behind him.

He tried to turn, but before he could swing around more than halfway, something hard and round pressed itself against the back of his neck. "Don't move, you son of a bitch," a man's voice shouted, "or I'll blow your damned brains out!"

Chapter 16

Longarm recognized the voice. It belonged to Hughey, the outlaw who had been tied up and gagged and placed in the shed earlier by Doc Barkley. A second later, Hughey confirmed his identity by saying, "I didn't think I'd ever get loose from them knots. Damn that old bastard for tyin' me up so tight!"

Longarm heard other voices approaching, calling questions. Culhane and his men had heard Hughey's shout and were coming around the house to investigate. In the blink of an eye, the odds had swung overwhelmingly against Longarm.

And there was nothing he could do to swing them back.

Culhane and several of his men burst around the corner of the house, guns drawn. Culhane stopped short at the sight of Longarm standing there. "You!" he exclaimed. "I was hoping that sandstorm got you and you were dead, but I figured you weren't, you bastard."

"I got him, boss," Hughey said excitedly, a grin on his face. "I got him just like you wanted. Now he won't never tell nobody about those wells out in the desert!"

"Shut up, you fool!" Culhane hissed, but the damage was already done. Hearing the commotion at the back of the house, Sarah had run through the kitchen to the rear door in time to hear Hughey's damning words. Longarm saw her jerk the door open with an expression of horror and stunned disbelief on her face.

"Marshal Long!" she said.

"Marshal?" Culhane said. "Sarah, what—"

Hughey turned a little, and the gun went away from Longarm's neck. "Boss?"

Longarm did the only thing he could. He threw himself forward through the open door, diving into Sarah and knocking her backward. Hughey's gun jerked back toward him and lanced flame from its muzzle as the outlaw triggered it. Culhane yelled, "No!" and fired at the same time, hammering a bullet into Hughey's body that knocked him backward to the ground.

Longarm kicked the door shut behind him as he rolled over, clawing for his gun.

Outside, Culhane shouted to his men, "Get back! Hold your fire, damn it! No shooting! Sarah's in there!"

Yes, she was, Longarm thought, and under other circumstances she would have been a vision of loveliness in her white wedding gown with the colorful desert rose pinned to the front of it. But now the veil was askew over her face as she came up on her hands and knees and stared at him. He could tell she hadn't been hit by Hughey's wild shot.

"Marshal Long?" she said. "You . . . you were telling the truth . . . about Brent?"

"You know I was," he told her as he kept his Colt trained on the back door in case Culhane and his men rushed it. "You heard what Culhane's man said."

"I . . . I can't believe . . ." Sarah gave a little shake of her head and then pushed the veil back so that her face was uncovered. She reached out and grabbed the Winchester that was leaning against the wall in the corner of the kitchen. As she came to her feet, she said in a voice

172

taut with tension but still strong, "I'll cover the front door."

A quick grin of admiration tugged at the corners of Longarm's mouth. Sarah Hodge was one hell of a woman. In a matter of seconds, her carefully ordered world had been shattered around her, but she was able to throw off that shock and do what needed to be done. "Stay low," Longarm told her. Crouching, he edged over behind the butcher-block table in the center of the kitchen, which was sturdy enough to provide some cover if shooting started. Sarah placed herself beside the doorway, with the barrel of the rifle thrust around the jamb so that she could fire down the hall toward the front door if she needed to.

The question now was what would Culhane do? His world had been turned upside down just as surely as Sarah's had been. His carefully orchestrated plan was in a shambles, because now Sarah would never marry him and he had to know that. Not only that, but the shooting that had already taken place would draw the attention of the townspeople. Probably someone was on the way to investigate the shots already. If Sheriff Hampton really had gone straight, would he try to stop Culhane? Or would he be sympathetic enough to his former partner to look the other way while Culhane and his men stormed the house and killed Longarm and Sarah? Hampton couldn't very well do that if he intended to stay in Bell City and continue wearing a badge, but there was no guarantee that he wouldn't decide to throw in with Culhane and go back on the owlhoot.

"I . . . I can't believe he lied to me all these months," Sarah murmured as she gripped the Winchester and kept the front door covered.

"That ain't all of it," Longarm said. "Doc Barkley was in on the deal, too. He was Culhane's silent partner."

Sarah glanced at him. "Doc? No! I . . . I've known him since I was a little girl."

"Folks change," Longarm said grimly. "He decided he wanted to be a rich man, and Culhane gave him that chance."

"What happened to him? Where is he now?"

"He tried to kill me once he got me out of town. His shot missed, though."

"You killed him." Sarah's words were a statement, not a question.

"Seemed like the thing to do at the time."

Sarah sighed. "I'm sorry, Marshal. I should have believed you from the first. Then maybe no one else would have had to die."

"Ain't no way we'll ever know for sure, but I wouldn't count on that, Miss Sarah. This lash-up was bound to come down to bullets sooner or later."

She didn't say anything. Longarm listened to what was going on outside, which seemed to be nothing. Culhane and his men were waiting out there; he was certain of that. He hadn't heard any hoofbeats, so he knew they hadn't taken off for the tall and uncut, figuring the jig was up and they'd be better off cutting their losses. Longarm had harbored a faint hope that was what would happen, but he didn't really expect it to.

Suddenly, he heard a new voice outside. Sheriff Hampton called, "Brent! What the hell's going on here?"

Feigning a note of frantic worry in his voice, Culhane answered loudly enough for Longarm to hear through the open window. "There's an outlaw holed up in Sarah's house, Clyde!" he said. "I was talking to her, and he bulled in the back and started blazing away! I . . . I think he may have shot her!"

Sarah gasped. "That liar!"

"Culhane's no fool," Longarm said in a low voice. "He's trying to salvage what he can from this mess. Now that Hampton's here, Culhane'll bust in and make sure there's enough lead flying around to get us both. Then he can convince Hampton I must've killed you. That way he can keep his ranch and the stolen cattle, even if he won't get all the land you own and that railroad spur line."

Sarah turned her head and stared at him as she tried to digest this new revelation about Culhane's plan. Obviously, she was having a hard time comprehending the full evil of the scheme.

"My God," she murmured. "I really was a fool, wasn't I?"

Longarm didn't make any reply. An idea had occurred to him, and he was busy tearing a strip of cloth off the tail of the shirt he was wearing. When he had it, he used one of the scalpels he had taken from Barkley's medical bag to bore a narrow hole through the cork that sealed the neck of the brown bottle containing ether. Still using the scalpel, he stuffed the strip of cloth through the hole, leaving a couple of inches dangling out.

"They'll likely come from both directions at once," he said to Sarah. "Can you shoot if you have to?"

"I can shoot," she replied, her voice flat.

"Even at Culhane?"

Sarah hesitated, but then she said, "I can do what I need to do."

Longarm hoped she meant it. He knew the showdown wouldn't be long in coming. Culhane couldn't afford to delay. That would just give Hampton and any other townspeople who were around the chance to ask questions and start wondering about what was really going on here. Culhane's only hope of coming out of this with anything was a massacre, and a quick one at that.

Outside, Hampton called, "Brent, don't do anything foolish . . . Brent, damn it, come back here!"

Longarm heard that and knew the ball was about to open again.

He pulled a lucifer from his pocket, snapped it into life, and held the flame to the makeshift fuse in the bottle of ether. Footsteps pounded on the front porch. When the strip of fabric was burning, he leaned out and rolled the bottle down the hall. It came to a stop a few feet away from the door, just as a couple of the rustlers burst through, shooting.

At the same instant, something slammed into the back door and knocked it open. Longarm rolled onto his belly, half-shielded by the table, and tipped up the barrel of his Colt. He fired at the first man through the door. A few feet away, Sarah's Winchester cracked.

Then, the highly volatile ether caught fire, and trapped as it was in the bottle, the result was a sharp explosion that sent glass and flame flying around the foyer. A man screamed as the blast caught him and flung him through the air.

The man who had come through the back door was knocked off his feet by the slug from Longarm's gun. The next man stumbled over him, giving Longarm the chance to send a bullet into his belly. He folded up and went down. That made two men out of the fight back here and at least one at the front door. How many men did Culhane have with him?

"Hold your fire! Hold your fire, you fools!" That was Sheriff Hampton bellowing outside.

Longarm risked leaning out from his cover to take a glance down the hall. The house was on fire, the blaze having been started by the ether explosion. If the fire spread very much, he and Sarah couldn't stay here. But could they risk going out yet? Where was Culhane? Had he rushed the house with the others? He wasn't one of the men Longarm had shot; the big lawman was certain of that.

"You inside the house!" Hampton shouted. "Come out with your hands up! The place is on fire!"

"Sheriff Hampton!" Sarah called. "Don't shoot! We'll come out!"

"Sarah!" Hampton sounded shocked. "Are you all right?"

"I'm fine!" She hurried over to Longarm and reached down to grasp his arm and help him up. Already clouds of black smoke were drifting into the kitchen, pulled through the house by the draft created by both doors being open. "We have to get out of here while we still can, Marshal."

Longarm nodded as he came shakily to his feet. He felt a pang of guilt over the fire. They might not have been able to hold off the rush of Culhane's men without the help of the explosion, though.

Coughing, both of them stumbled through the door and out of the smoke. Longarm still had the Colt in his hand, and Sarah was holding the Winchester. Longarm's eyes smarted from the smoke, blurring his vision. He blinked them rapidly and looked around for Culhane.

"Don't shoot!" Sarah called again to Hampton.

The lawman hurried up to them, a shotgun in his hands. "What the hell?" he exclaimed when he saw Longarm. The twin barrels of the greener swung toward the big lawman. "Drop that gun, you son of a bitch!"

"Sheriff, it's all right," Sarah said quickly. "This man is a U.S. marshal."

"What?"

Longarm lowered the Colt. Distractedly, because he was still looking for Culhane, he said, "That's right, Hampton. I'm a deputy marshal out of Denver. Where's Culhane?"

Hampton looked mighty confused. He didn't answer Longarm's question. Instead he turned and shouted to the townspeople who had gathered to stare in awe at the burning house, "Get a bucket brigade going!"

Longarm didn't think that was going to do any good. The fire was burning too strongly already. He felt dizzy, and his side was wet. This time, the bullet wounds *had* broken open again.

Culhane was nowhere in sight. He must have started his men rushing the house, then pulled back to see what was going to happen, Longarm thought. When Longarm and Sarah had turned back the charge and it became obvious that they might get out and talk to Hampton, Culhane must have slipped back to his horse and rode hell-for-leather away from Bell City. Longarm felt a pang of disappointment. He had wanted to see Culhane again over the barrel of his gun.

While the townspeople fought the fire, Hampton herded Longarm and Sarah past the body of Hughey and over to the shed. "Somebody's got one hell of a lot of explaining to do," the local lawman growled.

"It was Brent, Sheriff," Sarah said. "He was behind all of it. He'd been rustling cattle on the other side of the desert in Rampart Valley, and he tried to kill Marshal Long when the marshal found out about it. He was willing to kill me, too, rather than let me reveal what I'd found out about him."

Hampton frowned. "Damn it, that doesn't make any sense!" He gnawed at his lower lip. "But Brent used to be a wild one, all right. I know, because I was, too. I thought he'd settled down, though."

"I can lay all of the cards on the table for you, Sheriff," Longarm said. "Right now, though, I'm feeling a mite puny."

"Yeah, I can see you're bleedin'. We'd better find Doc Barkley and get you patched up again."

A humorless smile altered the rugged planes of Longarm's face. "Well, Sheriff, that's a whole 'nother part of the story you're likely going to have a hard time believing . . ."

• • •

A knock sounded on the door of Longarm's room in Bell City's only hotel. He called, "Come in." Under the sheet, his hand was filled with the butt of the Colt. A search of the town had turned up no sign of Culhane, even though the rest of his men had been found and arrested. Longarm thought the skunk was a long way from Bell City by now, but just in case Culhane was still around and wanted to take his vengeance on the man who had ruined everything for him, Longarm wasn't going to take any chances.

The door swung open, and Sarah Hodge stepped into the room. She wore a dressing gown borrowed from the wife of the hotel's proprietor.

Longarm grunted, took his hand out from under the sheet, and put the gun on the small table beside the bed, next to the lamp that was burning with its flame turned low. "I reckon you couldn't sleep, either," he said to Sarah.

She shook her head and closed the door behind her. "No. There are just . . . too many thoughts going through my head." She came over and gestured at the foot of the bed. "Do you mind?"

Longarm shook his head. "I'll be glad for the company."

He hurt all over and was utterly exhausted, but too much had happened for sleep to come easily. His wounds had been cleaned and bandaged again, this time by Sheriff Clyde Hampton. Though no sawbones, Hampton had patched up enough bullet holes in his time to be fairly proficient at it. Longarm figured he was going to survive.

Hampton had listened, too, while he was doing his makeshift doctoring. He had taken in all the details of the stories Longarm and Sarah told him, and then he had sent someone to retrieve Doc Barkley's body from the buggy where Longarm had left it. Another man had galloped south to Rossville with telegrams to be sent to Sheriff Willard over in Castleton and Chief Marshal Vail back in

Denver. With Sarah's testimony added to Longarm's, Hampton had had no choice but to accept the fact that Culhane and Barkley had been behind the rustling in Rampart Valley and had plotted to take over the land that the railroad would use for the new spur line.

After that, Longarm and Sarah had been brought here to the hotel and given rooms. To Longarm's surprise, the bucket brigade had saved most of Sarah's house, though there was quite a bit of damage to the structure. It would be a while before it could be fixed up and lived in again. For the time being, Sarah could live at the hotel, and Hampton had promised to keep Dobie at his office and take good care of the little dog. It looked like everything was going to end up just fine in Bell City.

Except for the fact that all of Sarah's hopes and dreams for the future had been destroyed.

After a while, though, Longarm thought as he looked at her now, there would be more hopes and dreams. She was strong enough to come through this.

She reached over and took his hand where it lay on top of the sheet. "Thank you," she said.

"For what? Coming in here and turning your whole blasted world upside down?"

"Do you really think I would have been happier married to a killer and an outlaw? Sooner or later, the law would have caught up to Brent. It would have been worse if I'd been his wife."

Longarm shrugged. "Maybe so. I'm just sorry things couldn't have worked out better for you." He paused, then added, "They'll be all right, though. There ain't a lick of doubt in my mind about that."

She smiled. "You're quite an amazing man, Custis. You took enough punishment the past few days to kill anybody else, but no matter how hurt and sick you were, you kept thinking and fighting." She moved farther up the bed, drawing closer to him. "Just how much strength do you think you have left?"

Longarm stared at her, his eyes widening. He burst out, "Lord, woman, what're you trying to do, kill me?"

Sarah laughed. "I was hoping you'd have the strength to hold me for a little while."

"Oh," Longarm said, abashed. "I reckon I could do that, all right. In fact, I'd admire to do that."

She slipped into the curve of his arm and snuggled against his unwounded side. With a sigh, she rested her head on his chest. "This was supposed to be my wedding night," she whispered. "But . . . I'm not going to think about that."

Longarm tightened his arm around her and said, "Best not to. Sometimes folks are better off just holding each other and not thinking at all."

Chapter 17

Longarm was sitting in Clyde Hampton's office a couple of days later, smoking a cheroot and chewing the fat with the local lawman, when Sheriff Stan Willard from Castleton walked in.

"Well, for somebody who got shot up, you look fit as a fiddle, Marshal," Willard said with a grin.

"Folks around here been taking good care of me," Longarm said, returning Willard's smile. "What are you doing over here in these parts, Sheriff?

"Came to see you," Willard replied. He shook hands with Hampton, then pulled up a chair. "I got that wire Sheriff Hampton sent me. Of course, I was about to bring a posse over here anyway."

Longarm frowned. "How come?"

"To help you round up Culhane and the rest of those rustlers, of course."

Longarm and Hampton exchanged a puzzled glance. Longarm asked the question that had both of them confused. "How did you know about that *before* you got the wire?"

Willard's grin got bigger. "Elizabeth Townsend told me."

Longarm sat up straight, the shock going through him like a bolt of lightning. "Elizabeth . . . ?"

"She's all right, Marshal," Willard said quietly. "Leastways, she will be once she recovers from the bullet hole in her shoulder. She got away that night when she was with you in the desert and got shot. Culhane thought she was dead, but she managed to crawl off and hide in some mesquites. Then later, that dun horse came along, and she was able to reach up and grab hold of a stirrup. She hung on, and he pulled her along until she got up the strength to climb up into the saddle. She made it back to one of the ranches in the valley the next day, and the folks there took care of her and sent for me."

"Good Lord," Longarm breathed, hardly able to believe what Willard was telling him. And yet, when he thought back on it, on more than one occasion, Culhane had referred to the person who had been with Longarm at the well as *"he"*. Culhane wouldn't have made that mistake if he had actually found Elizabeth's body and confirmed that she was dead. Culhane had been fooled into thinking that shot had killed Elizabeth—just as Longarm had been mistaken.

"As soon as you feel up to riding, we'll head down to Rossville and catch a train back over to Castleton," Willard went on. "I know Elizabeth would be mighty pleased if you stopped by to see her on your way to Denver."

"I'll do more than that," Longarm said. "I been shot. My boss Billy Vail will have to give me a little time off to recuperate. I reckon I'll spend it in Castleton." He glanced across the desk at Hampton. "Not that I don't appreciate everything the folks in Bell City have done for me."

Hampton waved a hand. "Don't worry about that, Marshal. And don't worry about Sarah. From what I hear, she's going to be pretty busy now that she's decided to prod the railroad into going ahead and building that spur line." He chuckled. "I figure before it's over, she's liable to be the first lady railroad tycoon in these parts."

That sounded just about right to Longarm, too.

He puffed on his cheroot for a moment, still almost overcome with emotion at the revelation that Elizabeth was alive and relatively well. Finally, he said, "You know, the one thing I'm sorry about is that Culhane got away."

Sheriff Willard thumbed back his hat and said, "Well, that's one more bit of news I've got for you. I wanted to get over here as fast as I could, so instead of going the long way around, I loaded up on canteens and came across the *Llano Caliente*. About halfway here, I found a man's body, and I reckon it was that fella Culhane. About thirty years old, blond hair, might have been handsome if he hadn't been dead?"

Longarm leaned forward tensely. "That's him. What happened to him?"

"From the looks of it, he died of thirst. He didn't have a canteen or anything to carry water with him. I've seen men who went that way before. It's not a pretty way to die, and you never forget what a fella looks like when that happens to him. A little ways farther on, I found his horse. Horse was dead, too. I figure it went down first, and Culhane tried to make it on foot."

Hampton said, "When he lit out from here, he must have thought that nobody would expect him to head across the desert. I sure wouldn't have, especially with no water."

"Wait a minute," Longarm said. "Why didn't he head for one of the wells he used to water those stolen cows?"

"I'm sure he planned to," Willard said. "That's why he didn't take the time to bring any water with him. But there's something else I discovered out there on the desert. Remember that sandstorm a few days back?"

Longarm nodded grimly. He remembered it, all right. Chances were, he would never forget it.

"Well, that sandstorm was so bad it filled in and covered up every one of those wells." Willard shook his head. "The *Llano Caliente*'s just as dry and deadly now as it ever was, and Culhane found that out the hard way."

Longarm drew in a deep breath, taking a bleak satisfaction in the way fate had caught up with Brent Culhane. Culhane had gone into the desert and found death . . .

Thinking of Elizabeth and Sarah, Longarm knew that *he* had gone into the *Llano Caliente* and found not one desert rose, but two.

Watch for

**LONGARM AND THE RANCHER'S
DAUGHTER**

291st novel in the exciting LONGARM
series from Jove

Coming in February!

Explore the exciting Old West with one of the men who made it wild!

JAKE LOGAN
TODAY'S HOTTEST ACTION WESTERN!